Total-E-Bound Publishing books by Catherine Chernow:

Diary of a Mad Escort

Anthologies:
Cougars and Cubs: Lucky in Love

HER ROMAN'S HAND

CATHERINE CHERNOW

Her Roman's Hand
ISBN # 978-0-85715-428-6
©Copyright Catherine Chernow 2011
Cover Art by April Martinez ©Copyright 2011
Interior text design by Claire Siemaszkiewicz
Total-E-Bound Publishing

Published in 2011 by Total-E-Bound Publishing, Think Tank, Ruston Way, Lincoln, LN6 7FL, United Kingdom.

Manufactured in the USA.

HER ROMAN'S HAND

Dedication

For my editor...Andrea Grimm

Chapter One

Lyla Thomas slowed her car, coming to a complete stop at another red light on the busy main thoroughfare running through Dennisport. The small town sat midpoint on Cape Cod, a perfect little summer vacation spot. As she drove, the hot sun beat down on the tarred road, creating a shimmering mirage. It looked as if a small pond glistened in the middle of the street.

While she waited for the light to turn green, she thought about everything she'd done so far. She had been whale-watching, she'd even experienced that crazy placed called Provincetown, where all the drag queens hung out, but her favourite New England coastal treat came to mind, quickly overtaking all her other memories...

Lobster roll.

She reached down and fingered the waistband of her shorts.

"Damn, they're tight," she muttered.

Inspiring and motivating people to change their lives was her sole support, but lately, it didn't fulfil her.

That's probably why she ate all that lobster roll.

It filled a void. Deep inside.

The light finally went from red to green. Lyla pressed her foot on the car's accelerator and drove down Route 28, her mind filled with ideas on what she could do to branch out on her own. She'd worked for BestUCanBe Corporation for the past ten years, allowing them to capitalise handsomely on her talent. They, in turn, fed her speaking engagements and seminars where she taught employees of major corporations to be the best *they* could be.

Bored.

Stifled.

Searching for more.

Those words rang in her head. She'd heard them many times, but now she had to admit that for the most part them came from...

Her.

She should be grateful she had a job in this lousy economy, she should be ecstatic that companies still wanted to hire her, but the truth stared her in the face. Lyla couldn't stand to hear one more person complain about their boss, co-workers and how much damn work they had to do and how tough it was to do it.

She truly enjoyed the last seminar she did on her own. She promoted it, sold it, and worked it all by herself, savouring the experience of a mixed audience who truly desired to change their lives for the better and not simply mewl about it.

Monotony was the enemy. It sapped her strength and drive like the most rampant disease. Maybe it would be fun to reinvent her stifling career.

Ever since she graduated from college, she'd been on her own. She'd had to fight with her parents to let her attend a non-catholic university. Grudgingly, they gave in, but her relationship with them had become strained over the years.

Then again, she was never quite the obedient child they had hoped for.

She didn't want to spend her entire young adult life in the confines of strict, religious-infused education. Lyla always fought for what she wanted, even as a kid. She had to otherwise, her parents would have mowed her down in their quest to make her into the perfect little person they thought she should be.

That battle continued into adulthood. She won, but at a high price.

If things didn't pan out, she couldn't go crawling back to Mommy and Daddy now.

She'd network her ass off if she had to. She'd supplement her income by waiting tables or pumping gas or anything she could get her hands on. Whatever she had to do to invigorate her own business as a motivational speaker.

She glanced at the sunny, blue, cloudless skies surrounding the Cape.

She had lots of thinking to accomplish. Tons of ideas to sort out.

At least she picked a wonderful location to do it in.

Lyla slowed the car to a halt at another red light. She tapped the steering wheel in time to the beat of the music coming from her iPod. Glancing around, she noticed a small house set back from the road.

She read the words on the sign over the door. "Hardin Books."

Strange.

She'd been up and down Route 28 many times since she'd arrived in Dennis. Why hadn't she noticed that particular store on her previous trips?

She could sit her ass on that beach chair the Crossair Resort provided, stick her toes in the water and read a good old-fashioned trashy novel.

It sounded like heaven.

She looked to her right and noticed no traffic. She made a sharp turn into the lane next to her then proceeded into the bookstore parking lot.

She got out, the heat assaulting her face like a hot stream of air from a blow drier. Sweat beaded on her upper lip. She swiped it with her fingers then walked inside the store, the bell above the door jangling.

Cool air surrounded her. A familiar, musty smell drifted by her nose—old paper and leather. Lyla remembered that odour from her childhood when she used to visit the local library. It wasn't unpleasant, in fact, it welcomed her and beckoned her further into the store.

She glanced at the few patrons milling about. Some of them seemed older than dirt. Their wrinkled, tanned faces spoke of much time spent in the sun. Perhaps they were locals. No matter, though, for they were intent on reading and didn't seem to notice her arrival.

Good!

She could browse the shelves brimming with love stories and not be bothered by unwanted company.

A slow smile spread across her face.

"Porn for women," she muttered under her breath, slipping her dark glasses down her nose to glance at the titles and racy covers.

Memories of her Catholic high school days surfaced. The Sisters of Perpetual Indulgence would have slapped her hands with a ruler if they knew what she read in secret.

"I'm a grown woman, damn it, I can read what I want." She glanced around, hoping no one heard. She hadn't meant to say that aloud. If she could just curb the impulse to say what was on her mind.

But old habits die hard.

No pun intended, sisters.

Half her problem during her religious school days stemmed from the fact that she always tried to best those stern old nuns. Lyla lost track of the countless times they wrote notes home to her parents.

Once, they almost expelled her. She had been eighteen then, and would graduate from high school in another few months. The notion that the nuns would toss her out with only a few months to go didn't sit well with her father. The good sisters had given him a choice. They would punish his wayward daughter, or...

She would be expelled from school.

Lyla's face heated when she thought about the beating she'd received, bent over the principal's desk. Sister Mary Rutherford had allowed Lyla to keep her panties on, but the humiliation and pain she suffered from that ruler never left her memory.

She browsed the shelves, looking at book after book, hoping to distract her mind from thoughts of that spanking. Damn, her clit pounded. It always did when memories of that punishment surfaced.

From across the room, a large tome caught her eye. It sat on a table, out in the open. It seemed old and worn. The light from above made a myriad of odd stones shimmer on the book's cover.

She walked towards the book, remembering how she had experienced the last laugh, enjoying the beating she received from the nuns. If they thought they could strike the insolence from her, they were sadly mistaken.

Once she discovered how much she enjoyed that spanking, she strove to break every rule possible.

Her mouth curved into a wry grin.

Her parents' generous donation is what enabled her to stay at school. The disgrace they'd suffer if their hellion daughter remained at home would devastate them.

Maybe that's why motivational speaking appealed so much to Lyla. She enjoyed helping people buck their fears. If you wanted to change your life, you had to break free and purge all those self-imposed rules and regulations from your mind.

Nothing changes if nothing changes.

She stopped by the table where the large, old book lay. Curious, she marvelled at the ornate, gilded cover. She struggled to lift it, realising it was better to leave it on the table.

She opened the unusual cover, imbedded with odd stones in many different colours.

Lyla read the words on the first page aloud, "Coitus more ferarum."

She looked around to see if anyone heard. Heads bent, eyes on the books in their laps, the few customers in the store besides Lyla seemed intent on reading. The rest continued to browse, undisturbed by her outburst. It appeared as though none of them understood any words she uttered.

Neither did she.

When she looked down at the page again, one word, written in English, appeared as if someone actually wrote on the yellowed paper in a kind of scrawl...*Seek.*

She snapped her brows together in thought, curiosity making her turn the page.

The good sisters of Perpetual Indulgence would have been shocked if they knew what she viewed next.

"Holy shit!"

That outburst got the bookstore patrons' attention. One by one, they lifted their heads, craning their necks while they scowled, annoyed that someone disturbed their leisure.

Lyla's eyes widened as they beheld a drawing.

A man and woman, dressed in clothing from a bygone era, were doing it 'doggie style', the woman's white tunic rucked up over her ass. It revealed just a glimpse of pussy between her legs.

Snap!

She closed the book, shaking her head, wondering why in hell the owner of the bookstore would leave in plain sight a volume filled with flagrantly pornographic pictures.

She read the title, "A History of our World Through Illustration."

She couldn't argue that it was *illustrated.* However, if that's what the author thought olden times entailed, they had another think coming.

She snuck another peek, inquisitiveness eclipsing her outrage as she read line after line of detailed description, but not of chronological details regarding major battles or events of long-gone days.

She whispered the words on the next page, "'First, the man must arouse the woman. This can be done in several ways. Some prefer slow stroking at the entrance to the woman's vallum'." She bit down on her lower lip while she concentrated. "Vallum," she said aloud. "Vallum," she repeated, tapping her chin in thought.

Lyla flipped to the next page, where she saw a pencil sketch of a woman, her legs spread, while she sat on a man's lap. His hand lay on her pussy.

In the next instant, realisation dawned, the meaning of the word that had eluded her becoming clear. "Vagina," she whispered. "That's what the hell *vallum* means." She shook her head and rolled her eyes. "Sisters, you'd have washed my mouth out with soap and made me write on the blackboard a hundred times, 'I will *not* be a naughty girl and look at dirty pictures'."

A warm, rich chuckle drifted by her ears. A deep, male voice followed. "You must have been a holy terror."

She turned abruptly, her nose colliding with a wide chest, covered by a snowy-white T-shirt.

She glanced upwards, her eyes meeting a sculpted, angular face that held the faintest shadow of a beard. Dark eyes locked with hers. Jet-black, wavy hair framed the handsome visage.

Lyla studied the man's nose, for it had an unusual, prominent, high bridge.

"I always try and guess which drawing the customer will like best." His eyes never left her face.

She squared off with him, for his large, smoky orbs held challenge, as if he dared her to look some more. Lyla never could resist a taunt.

He moved closer, his exotic scent intoxicating, a mix of citrus, mint, and a musky, male smell that Lyla could only describe as...him.

"The ancients had no qualms about depicting sex in all forms." He looked over her shoulder, his nearness unsettling. Her belly quivered in response.

Lyla turned the pages, the breath catching in her chest. She didn't know where her boldness rose from, while a sudden urge surfaced to view the book with this man.

One drawing depicted a woman, her dress hiked up around her hips, her bottom naked. A man stood behind her, beating her bare ass with what looked to be a wispy broom.

Lyla's body responded to the image, her pussy beating in time with her heart. She squeezed her legs shut to keep the throbbing at bay.

He turned the book slightly. Gazing at the illustration, he told her, "Ah, yes. That particular punishment device is an early form of a whip known as a 'flagrum'."

"Must've hurt," she muttered, her heart racing in response to the image before her.

He shook his head. "Not as much as the later version. *That* one had metal tips attached to the lashes." He peered at the drawing again. "What she's receiving is *fustigatio*. That's a beating for a minor offence—more like a spanking."

"Such archaic brutality. I can't believe men were allowed to do that."

He raised one dark brow. "Most ancient societies were patriarchal, filled with dominant alpha males." His voice dipped an octave. "Who, for the most part believed in chastising women the way that drawing depicts."

"What kind of society? I mean, what people?"

He glanced at the book again. "Judging from the type of whip, it could possibly be antiquated Roman times."

"It's brutal and humiliating." She tucked some hair behind one of her ears, but her hand shook. "I mean getting beat that way, it's embarrassing."

A corner of his mouth lifted. "That's the idea."

"No one should be whipped or spanked, especially women. We're not children, we're adults and we're too old to be—"

"A Roman man believes a woman is *never* too old to be spanked."

Heat crept into her face. "Are we uh, talking back then or now?"

"I'll leave you to guess at that. While you are, *I'll* try and figure out which illustration is your favourite."

She started to walk away, knowing her face had to be red as a beet.

What in hell possessed me to carry on such a stupid conversation? And with this total stranger!

"Let's see now," he mused aloud. "I'll bet you liked this last picture. The whipping. Pain and subjugation. Interesting. I would have never pegged *you* for that, but I must admit, I'm pleasantly surprised."

She turned around and lifted her chin, hoping she appeared confident when her legs turned rubbery. Her cheeks burned like the bright sun scorching the pavement outside.

"You're Lyla Thomas, aren't you?" he asked. "The one who gives all the seminars on changing your life?"

She nodded, realising that her dark glasses didn't hide her face well. She should have been thrilled that this guy recognised her, particularly since she wanted to revamp her career, but Cape Cod was supposed to be a quiet, little getaway vacation so she could figure out not just her job situation but also why her last three relationships were so fucked up.

She didn't need to get involved in another one, no matter how ruggedly handsome this man appeared to be.

And she didn't need annoying questions, or ridiculous discussions, or her head filled with notions about spanking.

Her body hummed, the pleasant sensation making her breasts heavy.

She removed her glasses and met Mr. Tall, Dark and Handsome's gaze with a cool look.

"Okay. You got me. I *am* Lyla Thomas."

His smile widened. "I attended your 'Get What You Want Out of Life' seminar. You changed *my* life."

"How so?" A tiny buzz of pleasure shot through her. *Flattery will get you everywhere.*

"Let's just say I left a very boring, very stale job to do what I really wanted, open a rare book store." He swept his hand out before him. "Welcome to Hardin Books." He bowed slightly. "Mark Hardin, bookstore owner and history student, at your service."

A vision of *him* servicing her pussy popped into her mind. He gave her another killer smile.

Drop dead sexy.

Lyla was a sucker for a good-looking guy.

Then again, that's what always got her in trouble. The gorgeous ones were full of themselves.

For once, she wanted a man to care about *her* needs.

She glanced at Mark's sculpted face. An unusual bump on his nose, combined with his high forehead and prominent cheekbones made him appear...noble.

She didn't think she knew anyone with a nose like that. She closed her legs to ward off a stirring sensation between her thighs. His damn nose made him look even more desirable.

Time to leave before I get myself in trouble.

"It's a wonderful book store and it's been nice meeting you." She turned on her heel.

"Don't go."

She stopped.

"That book you were looking at can take you on journeys to parts of yourself, of your mind and body, that you've been afraid to explore."

She turned around. He ran his index finger along her jaw. She shuddered pleasurably, the unexpected contact making her nipples pebble.

He dropped his hand, but it seemed as though he did reluctantly.

"The book is like an addiction." His voice dipped. "You can't stop looking at it. I understand. I feel the same way, too, it's just that—" He shook his head.

She angled hers. "It's like sneaking a look at the porn magazines your parents hid under their bed?"

The bell above the door jangled, signalling more customers.

He ignored the sound, lifting a brow instead. "Is that what you used to do?"

"I once found some under my mom and dad's bed. All their smug righteousness flew right out the window the day I discovered those magazines hidden there."

She gave a careless shrug, but inside, her nerves sizzled. The back of her neck prickled, as though something was about to happen. She pushed her crazy thoughts aside, choosing to concentrate on Mark.

"Where I come from, children don't have to sneak peeks, it's all over the place, in plain sight."

Her mouth dropped open in surprise. "Porn?"

"Let's just call them artistic renderings of a very natural part of life." He grinned.

"Where were you raised? In a brothel?"

"No, nothing as sordid as that." He seemed to hesitate for a few seconds before answering. "I've been living in America for a while. I go back home to visit occasionally."

"Where's home, then?"

He answered slowly. "Europe."

"Europe is a big place."

"My father travelled a lot on business, I did too, for a while. My family never stayed in one place too long."

Boredom slipped away while interest and curiosity took its place.

"Ah. Then you're a gypsy. Fascinating." She nodded. "Where are you from? Romania?"

"Well, actually, I'm—"

"Talk about quick assimilation. You have just a trace of an accent." She narrowed her eyes. "But then again, you could be pulling my leg."

"I never lie." His dark eyes bore into hers and reminded her of melted chocolate.

"Then you're a rare breed. Because most people lie on a constant basis. That's why they attend my seminars, so they can stop kidding themselves and come to grips with what they want in life."

"Aptly put."

"Is that why *you* came to my conference?"

"I went because your web page said you're not afraid of challenge. I figured if you changed *your* life for the better, I could do the same with mine."

"Glad I could help." She was a phony, knowing she pulled her own leg. It was easier to turn someone else's life around than your own. "So, tell me. What's the one thing I said that made you do such a turnaround?"

A thoughtful look graced his handsome visage. "'Nothing changes if nothing changes'."

She batted the air with her hand. "You could've got *that* off my Facebook page."

"Well then, how about this... 'No snowflake in an avalanche ever feels responsible'."

Her lips curved into a smile. "Very nice. You would have heard *that* if you came to my last seminar."

"I guess I had to stop viewing myself as one little ice crystal and start focusing on the larger outcome."

"May I ask you something?"

He nodded. "Of course."

"Why leave that old book out in the open, where everyone can see it? It looks like it's worth a fortune." She nodded towards the large tome.

"Did you pick it up?"

"Uh, yeah. Why?"

"Heavy, isn't it?"

"Someone strong enough could still carry it out of here."

"The security cameras would get them. They'd never make it out the door. There's a tracker on it."

"Oh, really? Where?" She raised a brow and glanced at the book.

He laughed. "I should tell you so you can thwart my security system?"

"I guess not." She returned his grin.

"It's my own invention. I patented a LoJack for rare books. All that, courtesy of your 'Get What You Want Out of Life' seminar."

"Now I think you really are pulling my leg."

"It's a marketing tool. I use it to sell books."

She shook her head in confusion. "What is?"

"That old tome. People are drawn to it. Usually, when a man looks at it, he immediately heads for the section on better lovemaking. He'll buy several books on the subject."

She rolled her eyes. "Right. Now I know you're really full of crap." She folded her arms across her breasts. "Like guys care about what women like."

"You'd be surprised," he murmured.

Her body responded to his deep voice. She was glad she had her arms across her breasts so he wouldn't see how the honeyed sound made her nipples peak.

"And what happens when a woman looks at that old tome?"

"She heads straight for the 'Romance' section." He winked.

"Sure they do."

"You, on the other hand, did the exact opposite. You were in that section when the book caught your eye."

"You've been watching me all this time, haven't you?"

"It's a small store. I don't miss a thing."

She wanted to explain. Pushing some hair behind one ear, she said, "I enjoy old things. That book looked like an antique."

"So it is."

"I was drawn to it, just as you said earlier." She angled her chin, the need to challenge him growing.

A corner of his mouth lifted. "You don't have to make excuses for your interest. It's fine. You're the first person to do the exact opposite of what I expected and that's refreshing."

"But—"

"Do you always argue?" His smile widened.

"I didn't know we were."

"It will be interesting to see who wins."

"I will." She raised her chin a fraction, feeling like a petulant child, her need to debate growing.

"I doubt it, but then again, winning isn't everything. It's in the losing, the submission, that makes life exciting."

What would it be like to submit to him?

Lyla kept her jaw at a defiant angle, but inside, her stomach fluttered. It mixed with curiosity, sending a zing of desire to her clit. It throbbed violently.

He remained where he was, looking at her, his heated gaze making her want to jump his bones. She swiped her damp palms against her thighs.

The loud jangling of the bell above the door broke the tension between them.

Mark glanced at the people that walked in.

"Go help your other customers." Lyla nodded, making a split-section decision. She didn't want to leave the bookstore or him. "I'm not going anywhere."

He smiled. Her heart did a strange little flip in her chest.

"We could grab a meal together later, if you'd like," Mark stated. "I'd love to tell you what your seminar really did for me." He angled his head. "We could discuss other things, too." His voice dropped. It sounded positively wicked. "Like why you enjoy looking at that last picture in the book."

"We'll just see about that meal."

Her pulse quickened. What would he really think about her if they ventured into that part of her kinky self?

Can I trust him?

"If you did agree to join me for dinner, what would you like to eat?"

"What did you say?" She bit down on her lower lip.

He reached out and tapped her nose. "We were discussing dinner. You know, the last meal of the day. Otherwise known as food-you-can-share-with-another-person. Preferably me."

"Oh, right. Dinner. Well..." Again she hesitated.

"If you'd rather not, I understand."

She reached out and grabbed his upper arm before he could walk away.

He looked down on her hand. "I'm not going anywhere, either, Lyla." Then his eyes slowly travelled upwards, ending on her face. "I'd be crazy to."

Damn, if she blew this, she might as well just give up on the opposite sex altogether. He was the smoothest, sexiest man she'd met in a while.

He was fascinating.

Oh, crap, just be honest! You want to screw his brains out.

"Mexican, or maybe Chinese. I like Hunan style," she told him.

"Ah, so you like your food hot and spicy. Interesting."

She rolled her eyes. "Chinese food is not the most exciting thing in the world."

"But you are."

She stilled.

"I'd venture to even say you like your food hot and spicy because it is controlled exposure to low-level discomfort."

"Huh?"

"It's something called 'benign masochism'. You get an endorphin burst from eating things like Chile peppers."

Her stomach rumbled. Lunch had been two hours ago. She imagined eating General Tso's chicken, and a hot pepper lining her tongue, its spicy goodness heating her throat.

"Perhaps I'll take you up on that dinner."

"I close the store at six. We could go after that. Where are you staying? I'll pick you up."

"How about I just meet you?"

"Okay, I'll see you at Choi's. Know where it is?"

"Yes," she murmured.

"Good, then I look forward to getting to know you." He strode towards a customer waiting at the counter, but not before hesitating for just a second.

Lyla would have sworn that he seemed as if he wanted to stay with her.

I'm reading too much into this...

She anticipated what a 'discussion' would be like with him during their dinner. They wouldn't be doing too much *talking* if she had her way.

Maybe that's what she needed — a good, hard fuck from a drop dead, gorgeous guy. Why bother with a relationship?

Besides, why sit on the beach in the hot sun with a book so she could fantasise about a man like Mark Hardin, when she could have the real thing?

She gazed at the small table where the antique book lay. One of the gems embedded in the tarnished gold cover glittered in the light overhead. The stone possessed an unusual colour — orange, with deep red tones. Lyla thought its shape resembled an hourglass, wider on top, narrower in the middle, then it expanded again on the bottom.

She walked back over to the book and lifted it from the table. This time, the old tome didn't feel quite as cumbersome as before, enabling her to run her fingers across the strange, hourglass-shaped gemstone. She stroked it, her fingers sliding down its smooth, highly polished surface.

She opened the book and snuck another peek at the picture of the woman being whipped. Mark's eyes caught hers from across the room. Her moxy surfaced. Lyla pointed to the picture, holding the book up so he could see it. A corner of his sensual mouth lifted in a wry grin.

Her pussy dripped, soaking her panties.

Just her luck to find Mister Right on the final day of her vacation.

She closed the book and clutched it tightly to her chest, enjoying her daydream about Mark when her hands tingled. Lyla tried to put the book down, but it wouldn't budge.

It seemed as if it were glued to her hands and chest.

A sense of urgency filled her body, as though time slipped by…quickly.

Something made her glance at her watch. It was three in the afternoon. In the next instant, the hands went crazy. They spun counter clockwise on the timepiece's white face.

They wouldn't stop. She tapped the face, thinking something must be wrong with it.

The hands continued to fly backwards, picking up speed as they raced across the dial.

Her feet grew numb. She couldn't feel the floor beneath them while at the same time she succumbed to dizziness. She swayed on her feet, but couldn't keep her balance.

The bookstore faded, the shelves melting away before her eyes.

"Lyla!"

She heard Mark call her name, but she couldn't form a response. He seemed so far away, his tall form blending into the fading scenery.

The room whirled around then a wide hole opened beneath her feet. She fell headfirst down a long, dark abyss, her body sliding towards a pinprick of light that shone in the distance. It grew larger, the closer she came.

What seemed like seconds later, Lyla could feel the ground under her feet again. When she looked upwards, she expected to see that vortex of spinning darkness but a half dome of concrete met her gaze.

She moved away, fearful that it might fall on her, yet she noticed that a crowd stood beneath it. People chatted with each other, casually lounging against walls constructed from stone. Those walls appeared to support the dome above their heads. Some people had arms laden with baskets filled with vegetables and rustic looking breads. Others carried earthenware jugs by their sides as they walked.

"Okay, if this is a joke, you got me," she said aloud.

She looked around, hoping to see Mark. In return, she received curious stares from the passersby.

When she glanced at her watch, both hands were stuck on the number ten.

Ten at night? She glanced upwards. Light filtered in through the dome.

It had to be ten o'clock in the morning...

How could it now be ten o'clock in the morning? Minutes ago, in the bookstore, it had been three in the afternoon.

When she glanced at her watch again, the hands on the dial moved, but now, they were both on the number twelve.

It just didn't make sense.

She was disoriented, as if a veil covered her mind. She slipped the watch from her wrist and shoved it in her shorts' pocket. It was no use to her if it couldn't give her the correct damn time.

It would be a cold day in hell before she spent a bundle on a designer watch again.

Hair clung to her cheeks, the hot, humid air making her tresses damp. She still clutched the book to her chest. Unease filled her, making her perspire. Tiny droplets of sweat inched their way down her face.

"Where am I?" she asked, her voice echoing. Lyla grabbed the arm of a woman walking by. "Pardon me, but could you tell me where I am?"

The woman looked down at Lyla's hand then muttered something unintelligible. She walked away, shaking her head.

Lyla then joined the throng of people gathered by something that looked like a busy shop.

Maybe, I can get some answers there...

Inside the store the walls were decorated with beautiful mosaic tiles. Fruits and vegetables lay in baskets that lined the floor. People milled about, gazing at the variety of food, talking amongst themselves. She received more strange looks, but then the people would go about their business.

She walked down the open corridor, where she passed what appeared to be more elaborately decorated stores that sold things like wine, oil, nuts, and cloth. Some shops even looked like a strange version of a 'take-out' restaurant, where peopled munched on meats, bread, and cheese as they exited. Most stores were just barrel-vaulted cubicles with a large opening to the street. The shops' interiors fascinated her, their beautiful mosaics depicting what was sold within.

What part of Cape Cod is this?

Above her head, the high domed ceiling that covered the marketplace allowed light to filter in while protecting her from the sun's brutal rays. She continued to walk, hoping to find the bookstore…and Mark.

When she did, she'd give him hell! His practical joke didn't amuse her in the least.

The longer she walked, the more she was convinced that the Cape seemed a world away.

Her knuckles whitened from the grip she had on the tome, but each time she attempted to release it, that strange, tingling sensation shot through her fingers. The book seemed as if it were cemented to her hands.

She walked the long corridor to encounter the market's end.

Frustrated, she went outside onto the busy street where she was bumped and jostled along with the crowd. She continued on, her feet hurting, her thin-soled flip-flops no match for the rough stone pavement.

She didn't know how long she walked, but the more she continued the thirstier she became. Her throat was dry and scratchy, making her feel as if she gulped sand.

Fatigue washed over her. The damn book weighed a ton. If she could put it down somewhere, maybe she could rest on a bench or…

Her dry throat suddenly closed. She struggled to get air into her lungs, gasping for each breath.

Lyla fought against something clamped over her mouth and nostrils. In the next instant, she was lifted from the pavement and tossed high in the air, her abdomen connecting with a hard, pointy object.

She heard several male voices. One of them spoke... "Corvus ero commodo."

Crude laughter drifted by her ears.

She viewed the street as it whizzed by, her eyes staring down at sandals attached to large, hairy feet. Lyla grew woozy from her precarious position hanging over what she now knew was someone's shoulder.

A hand crept up her shorts.

Her face heated when a rough pinch clipped the inside of her thigh, but Lyla wouldn't let him get the best of her. She kicked out her legs and screamed. "Help me! Someone help!"

The man jostled her against his shoulder, stopping abruptly. Another man lifted her head, bunching several strands of her hair in his fisted hand. He pulled her tresses until his face was in line with hers. Then he looked directly into her eyes.

His breath smelt foul. The few teeth in his mouth were black and rotted. One of his eyes was shut, a jagged scar crossing his lid down to his right cheek. His gravelly voice held low, menacing tones. "Per, meretricis."

The one thing she could decipher from his words was that the people in the marketplace spoke the same way.

It suddenly didn't matter.

The evil glint in that kidnapper's one, good eye made her grateful she couldn't understand a damn thing he said.

Chapter Two

Time passed lazily.

Outside, a bright orange ball of sunshine hung in the sky waiting for the second it could dip. Slowly, it started its descent, signalling midday's end and the start of late afternoon. The glaring rays sought a more western exposure, trickling into a spacious, open courtyard.

It warmed and nurtured the plants that grew there in clay pots, sheltered from the wind's hot breath by a canopy. Rooms with doors and latticed windows opened onto the yard. Streams of sunlight slipped through the small, wooden openings of the lattice, seeking their next resting place.

Soon, the sun's soft glow settled on a man who lay on the marble floor, his body curled into a foetal position. Heat stroked his face, making tiny sweat beads appear on his forehead.

He cracked one eye open and looked around.

Click! Clack!

It seemed as though animal hooves beat against the pavement yet, he knew that his bedroom adjoined the courtyard. It shielded him from the harsh sounds coming from the outside world.

Click.

Clack.

Again, he heard the sounds, but this time they grew steadily in his brain, until he was forced to place his hands on his head. The din rose. He clamped his hands over his ears, hoping to shut it out completely.

Sharp pain knifed through his skull. He turned his head slightly, but now, a band of soldiers marched though his brain, their steady footfalls beating a loud, staccato rhythm against his skull.

The door to his bedroom slid open. Footsteps echoed on the tile.

"Master, I've brought you refreshment. Even though it is late, cook said you should eat and..."

He cast a furtive glance at the person that just walked in, lifting a hand to shield his eyes from the sun's bright glare.

"Master? Why are you on the floor?"

I have no idea... He snapped his brows together in thought. Maybe he wound up on the floor because he'd had too much damn wine last evening.

But I didn't go out.

He uncurled his cramped arms and legs and rose on shaky feet.

Or did I?

A rank smell drifted by his nose. His stomach roiled, nausea swirling inside his gut. He certainly *felt* like he had imbibed too much wine.

A young woman smiled at him. She held out a large, heavy-looking platter. "I've brought you a delicacy. Stuffed dormouse."

His eyes widened at the sight, bile rising in his throat. He gagged then backed away, but she thrust the serving tray at him.

He wanted to push it aside, but toppled it to the ground instead. The food landed on the floor in a soggy heap of bread, meat and...

"*That* is my meal?" He pointed at the tiny animal carcass on the floor, then screwed his face into a grimace.

"Cook made it especially for you." She bent down, then picked up the small rodent the by the tail. "It's stuffed with pepper and nuts and some mouse meat."

He started to gag again. "Get that thing away from me!"

"Y-yes, Master."

She cleaned up the mess on the floor, dumping it back on the tray.

"M-Master?" Her eyes widened. "Why are you dressed that way?"

He looked down to see azure coloured material covering him from his waist to his ankles. The heavy material hugged each leg, unlike his usual clothing.

How did he come to be dressed in such an odd manner? *Think. Think, damn it!*

His memory stirred. He had pitched headlong through a black void. The dark tunnel seemed to have no end, for he travelled down its long slope, his body bouncing against the stone sides.

"Master?"

"What?"

"Your legs. What is...?"

The word was on the tip of his tongue. If he could just remember it...

In the next instant, the proper name for his attire sprang forth.

"They're called 'pants'." Another word popped from his mouth. "Jeans."

She pointed to his chest. Her finger brushed the linen of what he remembered was his 'shirt'.

"I'm sorry!" She bowed her head and stepped away, her body shaking. "I-I did not mean to touch you. Please don't punish me."

"For the love of — Appia, stop crying." He took the empty tray from her hands and placed it on a table, but his hands shook.

Why can I remember this girl's name, yet, I cannot recall other events?

She lifted her eyes to his chest. "What is *that*?"

"It is called a 'T-shirt'." He looked down at the white cloth covering his chest. "I'm quite sure that's what it is, a 'T-shirt'."

She nodded and replied, "Tuh shart."

"T." He repeated.

"Tuh."

He shook his head. "No. Look at my mouth. See how my lips are moving? It is teeeeeeeee shirt."

"Tuh. Shart."

"Just take the platter." The stench of stuffed dormouse filled his nostrils. "And go."

"I will get you an ornator." She grabbed the large plate.

He shook his head. "No! I don't need *anyone*. Now, go, please."

"But how will you ready yourself?" She gazed at his clothing, a puzzled look on her face. "Is that how you will be dressed?"

He took her by the upper arm and led her to the door. "I will manage." *While I try to figure out what happened to me!*

She placed a hand on the door, turning her head slightly. He noticed the faded purple bruise on her left cheek.

"Appia," he said quietly, lifting her chin with his index finger. "What happened to your face?"

"I, uh, walked into something," she mumbled.

"What?"

She inhaled sharply when he reached out and touched the purplish bruise.

"Did someone strike you?"

"N-no."

He gripped her shoulders between his hands. "I want the truth."

"Servius punished me."

Servius…who in hell was Servius?

"I-I was not fast enough this morning. Your breakfast was ready and I—" She burst into tears. "My leg aches me today. It is not easy to move."

He suddenly recalled that she aggravated this Servius person quite frequently, her tardiness a constant complaint. He glanced at the young girl. She was young, her pretty face still forming into a woman's beautiful countenance.

While he could push aside this Servius' constant protests, he could not turn away from the man's obvious abuse.

"Servius will not strike you again. I promise."

"Yes, Master."

"Put a cold cloth on your face and rest. If anyone questions why you're not working, tell them to see me."

She exited his bedroom. He slid the door closed behind her, turning to lean his back against it. Scrubbing a hand over his face, his fingers slid across something hard and bumpy.

Glancing into a polished, metal mirror, he noticed that an egg lined his forehead. The bump was the size of a large, gold coin. When he pressed a finger on it, pain sliced through his skull.

His head spun.

How did I acquire such a lump?

A mental veil covered his brain, his thoughts murky and unsettled. Then the cloak covering his mind lifted bit by bit.

His memory stirred. He had fallen down a long tunnel, bumping his head against the side. Maybe he had dreamt about that threshold and his journey last night, but the aches and pains blooming in every part of his body made him rethink that.

He changed into different clothing, something he deemed more appropriate.

From the corner of his eye, he noticed a small piece of metal on the floor near his bed. Walking towards it, he retrieved what appeared to be a small vessel. Running his finger across the smooth metal tin, he registered a memory.

His head had ached some time ago. So did his body. He had contracted an illness in a strange land he'd visited.

The 'flu'.

Using his thumbnail, he placed it beneath the tin's cover. It popped open, revealing the contents. Small, white tablets lined the inside. He remembered placing two white tablets in his mouth when his head and body hurt. A little while later, the pain had vanished.

"Ty-le-nol," he read aloud from the words on the vessel. "Temporarily relieves minor aches and pains."

The band of marching soldiers still trekked through his head, so he popped two small pills in his mouth, washing them down with water from a nearby pitcher.

He strode from his bedchamber and walked down a hallway, glad to know that his brain was starting to clear a bit.

At least he knew where he was going! If he kept walking, he'd wind up in an elegant hallway lined with marble. Everything in this damn place seemed to be constructed with that stone.

Did I do all that? I don't remember...but I must have good taste.

"Good morning, Excellency." A small man greeted him and bowed. He rose to his full height of five feet, five inches. "Are you all right, Excellency?" He pointed to the egg.

Desperation filled him.

Who is this man? Why does he know me?

In the next instant, his memory came to life. "Decimus!" he shouted. "Decimus." He grabbed the little man's hand and pumped it enthusiastically. "My old friend, Decimus."

He shook Decimus' hand so hard that the little man's body shook.

Decimus just stared at him, his eyes wide. "Friend?"

"Why, yes, I..." Why was Decimus questioning him? They were friends; they had to be. He had such fond feelings for the small fellow.

"I am your steward, Excellency." Decimus extricated his hand, took a step back, and bowed.

"Of course." His cheeks burned with embarrassment. *My steward.*

"Excellency, are you sure you're not ill?"

"Yes, I'm fine, Decimus. I took some Tyle — "

"You did what, Excellency?"

"Nothing," he replied, not wanting to go into long-winded explanations. If he couldn't understand what happened to him, how could he expect Decimus to? Besides, he was glad he remembered who this little old man was — a trusted servant. "Prepare my conveyance, I'm going out."

The skin on the back of his neck prickled. That same tingling sensation travelled down his arms. A strange, restless exigency filled him, the need to get out surpassing all others.

Perhaps he needed fresh air to clear the cobwebs in his mind.

Maybe then he could remember what happened.

* * * *

A little while later, he travelled through the city. The roads teemed with people, slowing his journey.

What made him leave his home?

And where should he go?

A black cloud hovered over his mind. Sadness so profound, so utterly devastating filled him. Perhaps it was that bump on his head. He fingered it again, the swollen, tender spot making him wince. That was probably the reason his emotions swayed from contentment to this edgy gloom.

He tried to distract himself from his morose thoughts, choosing to think about other words to describe the transports he used when he journeyed in that far-off land he visited.

One was called an automobile.

Three words came to the forefront of his mind... "Fully air conditioned," he said aloud, remembering that it meant 'cool air'.

Sweat trickled down his chest, the intense heat making his clothing stick to his body. He wouldn't mind a bit of that 'air conditioning' right now.

As his eyes closed, his mind filled with odd thoughts. He wanted to go back to that fascinating land.

But how do I get there? I know I can, yet, I can't remember.

Frustration made him grind his fist into his thigh, for his brain was still locked behind a closed door in a room filled with memory.

Slowly, he pushed on the entrance. The door opened, revealing reminiscences of a flaxen-haired woman. She possessed hair the colour of the pale wheat that grew in the fields. His body grew hot, his erection making him uncomfortable. He shifted on the seat, feeling as if he needed to relieve his sudden desire for her.

His damned cock begged for only *her* touch.

He should punish her for doing this to him, for making him want her to the point where no other female would do.

Damned woman!

She must be a figment of his imagination, for she resembled a nymph.

Maybe, he scratched his head, he had lost his mind completely. His head started aching again. He pressed a thumb and forefinger against the bridge of his nose.

The flaxen-haired woman crept back into his thoughts, her image crystallising in his brain. She stood by a table, her eyes widening while she viewed the salacious illustrations...

His eyes snapped open as memories spewed forth, the entrance now widening to the one spot in his brain where recollections were kept.

He hadn't been able to stop the catalyst she set in motion. He had followed her in a frantic attempt to stop the fierce energy flow propelling them backwards, but she fell too far down the tunnel for him to grab her.

It had been no dream nor any demented thinking on his part.

He slumped in his seat, disturbed that he hadn't been able to protect her while she made her perilous journey.

Was she scared? Hurt?

The idea that she was a living, breathing woman hit him full force, making his head spin. He had to try to find her before someone else did. Who knew what would happen if she were lost in the city.

He stuck his head through the window and shouted a command. "Subsisto!"

The vehicle came to a halt.

He got out and ran into the crowd, the blazing sun beating down on his head. He stopped suddenly, sliding a hand through his hair. Where should he look for her? The city was huge. It would take an eternity to find her, *if* she was even here.

Decimus caught up with him. "Excellency, wait!"

He turned around when he heard Decimus. What could he say without the wily man thinking that he had become deranged?

Dreams and actuality swirled together in his mind. He was positive he had gone insane, for it was hard to tell the difference between the two.

He was becoming more like his damn father every day.

As he ran down the street, hearing Decimus' call, one thought stayed in his mind. He had to find the woman of his dreams.

The woman who made them stark raving reality.

Chapter Three

Lyla's abductors carried her through winding streets and narrow alleyways.

Her captor's arm banded her thighs, his grip like iron. The more she struggled, the tighter his hold became.

She had a limited view, and from the little she could see and hear, the small street they were on was deserted, except for them.

Her heart plummeted. *How will I ever retrace their steps or get an idea of a landmark?*

The man's pointy shoulder dug painfully into her gut. The other men noticed her upturned backside. Their voices rose in crude laughter when one captor slapped her ass.

She sucked in a breath when her abductor's hand crept up her shorts, his fingers skimming the juncture between her thighs. She kicked out her legs and twisted, but all that got her was another stinging slap, this time on the back of her thighs.

Her kidnappers ran down narrow steps, their sandaled feet clacking on the rough pavement. In the next instant, Lyla's eyes grew accustomed to near-darkness. She managed to lift her head to see that light flickered softly on the walls. They appeared dirty and stained.

Perhaps her imagination shifted into overdrive, but she could have sworn the dark smears on the walls resembled dried blood splatters.

She forced down the bile rising in her throat, but she gagged on her own saliva. Sweat inched down her back. There was no moving air in the narrow corridor.

A powerful stench, like rotting meat, filled her nostrils.

She heard a creaking noise then the man carrying her tossed her from his shoulder. Lyla managed to stay upright, but she swayed on her feet.

When the room stopped spinning, she noticed a man sitting behind a wooden table. He had short-cropped hair and dark, beady eyes, reminding her of a crow or a…

Snake.

He rose to his feet and walked around the rough-hewn furniture. She trembled, for he carried a mean-looking whip in his hand. He stood before her, using the lash's hand to push her chin upwards.

One man addressed him, hesitation in his voice. "Es vos c-commodo, Corvus?"

Oh, how she wished she could understand them. The one thing she could discern was that the man with the whip was in charge.

He released her chin, a smile spreading across his face. He hooked his hand on her tank top, his fingers tugging it down between her breasts.

She screamed, the shrill sound echoing through the room.

The men laughed.

"Stop it." She pushed and shoved at the hand on her chest, but the man had an iron hold. "Oh, God, someone help me!" Her cries for help made them laugh more.

She heard a sound like cloth tearing. When she looked down, she realised that he had ripped her tank top from the neckline down to her waist. It gaped open, revealing her skimpy, strapless bra. It barely covered her breasts.

He stared at her brassiere, confusion lining his pudgy face.

"Quis est?"

He angled his head, studying her, then reached out to capture one of her breasts in his hand. She slapped it away, her body shaking.

His mouth tightened, his eyes narrowed. Then he ripped her bra, tearing the lacy cups in two.

Lyla stood before the men, her naked chest on display. She gathered her shredded bra and tank top, trying desperately to cover her nakedness.

He grabbed her by her hair and pulled her forward then fondled her breasts, roughly pinching her nipples.

She fell to her knees. The other men laughed, the sound grating on her nerves and dignity. The man with the whip wrenched her to her feet. He looked her right in the eyes while he pinched her breasts.

Anger suddenly replaced her earlier emotions. It rose to the surface, making her face contort with rage.

"Fuck off!" Lyla yelled, then spat at him.

Her spittle landed on his nose and chin.

She saw him raise his lash, and flung her arm across her face to shield it. The whip's tip dug into the soft, fleshy part beneath her upper arm.

She slid to the ground, cupping the wound he'd inflicted while sharp, hot pain knifed through her.

One man pulled her to her feet. Then two of them shoved and pushed her from the room, and down a narrow corridor.

The final humiliation came when they forced her into a cage. The bars rattled, then she heard the scraping of metal against metal.

They shackled her hands to the bars, making sure her arms remained above her head so they could view her half-naked form.

In the distance, she heard moaning and crying. The sounds tore at her heart. When her eyes adjusted to the inky darkness, she could make out other women chained inside cages just like hers.

The sobs grew louder.

Then she realised...

They came from her.

* * * *

"Excellency, wait!" Decimus grabbed his master's arm, bringing him to a halt. *I cannot allow my master to carry on this way. He will be the talk of the city for days to come.*

A fierce, protective feeling rose inside Decimus. It had always been there, ever since his master was a boy, but now, the stakes were higher. His master was full grown and heir to a large fortune, a fortune many would attempt to steal if they knew his master had gone insane.

"Excellency, you are running through the streets like a madman. Why?"

"I need to find a woman, Decimus. *Now.*"

Decimus' shorter legs doubled their pace to keep up with his master's longer strides. "Is that all?" Decimus rolled his eyes. "Why didn't you say so in the first place?" He pulled him aside. In a low voice, he said. "If you want a woman, I will secure one for you. Just tell me the price and description and I'll—"

"Not *that* kind of woman, Decimus. I'm looking for a particular one, with long, pale hair. About this high." He raised his hand, palm down, right near Decimus' head. "She's about your height."

Decimus' eyes scanned the crowded street. "I will do as you bid, but let's not stand here discussing it. You're already getting some very curious looks since you took off running."

"Decimus, I don't have time to waste. I need to search for her. This woman is special, she's—"

"I understand, Master." Decimus gripped his arm and drew him inside a dimly lit tavern, where groups of loud, boisterous men diced and gambled at small tables.

Half-naked women strode around with goblets, their heavy breasts swaying from side to side. They served the patrons of the dingy tavern, but never took their eyes from Decimus and his tall companion.

"We can talk in here, Master."

"I don't want to talk! I need to find this woman. It's important."

Decimus signalled a serving girl. "Wine," Decimus ordered. "For my master and me." He tossed a few coins on the table.

She scooped them up and gave a saucy wink, then walked away. A few minutes later, she returned with two goblets and placed them down on the table.

"Is she to your liking?" Decimus queried.

She turned on her heel and walked away, but gave a backward glance over her shoulder.

The master gazed at her retreating back and shook his head. "You don't understand." He took a sip from his cup and spat out a dark liquid stream. "This wine is horrible, Decimus." He plunked the goblet down on the table.

Decimus' eyes darted around the room. He lowered his voice. "We're not here for the, uh, excellent vintage, Master."

"I'll say." He wiped his mouth with the back of his hand.

"We're here so that we can have privacy while you explain everything to me."

That earned Decimus a dark look from the master.

"Excellency, I need to understand so that I may get you what you desire."

He sighed. "It's not what I desire, it's what I need to do."

"Of course." Decimus' mouth lifted in a knowing grin.

"This is useless." The master rose to his feet. "I'm leaving. If you'd like to help, fine. Otherwise, go home."

Decimus pulled him back down into the chair, surprised at his own strength despite his age. A sour look filled the master's face. He stayed in the chair, but it seemed as though he did so reluctantly. The master's shoulders slumped.

"Master, why do you look so troubled?"

He lifted his head, his eyes bleak. "Decimus, I need you to swear to me that what I'm about to tell you will stay in the strictest confidence." The master spoke in a hushed tone.

"It will, Excellency. You can trust me."

The master blew out a breath. "I thought I could fool myself, but no more." He glanced at Decimus, lowering his eyes. "You must think me very strange."

Decimus shrugged. "I cannot say."

"I wish you would. This is a time for truth, not mincing words."

"All right, then let me say this—you *have* been acting odd. Not just today, but for a long time. You disappear for days, sometimes months."

The master scrubbed a hand over his face. "For a while, I thought I dreamt things, but now I realise these places I've been to do not spring from my imagination. I've actually been to them."

Silence stretched between them. Then Decimus spoke. "I had a similar conversation once, with your father."

He looked at him sharply. "You did?"

"When you were a little boy, your father used to leave your mother, and you, for long periods of time. He claimed he travelled all over the empire on business, but one day, I found him in straights similar to yours." Decimus nodded. "He wound up back home dressed in odd clothing."

"That happened to me this morning."

"I know, Excellency."

The master's brows rose.

"Nothing escapes me, Excellency. I served your father in the same capacity as I serve you now. My knowledge gives me power—the power to aid you. The more I hear and know, the more I can assist you."

"I came back dressed in that strange attire because I didn't have time to prepare myself properly to journey back home." He lowered his eyes. "I, uh, was distracted."

Decimus leant back in his chair. He folded his arms across his chest and grinned. "By this woman you're so determined to find?" *I'd like to meet her—this woman, one tiny female who holds my master so enthralled.*

"She slipped through the portal."

Decimus snapped his brows together. "What is this 'portal'?"

"It is an opening, a way into the future...and the past." He continued on, the words spilling quickly from his mouth, "You get to the future, or the past, by stroking a stone embedded in something called a 'book'."

Decimus rubbed a hand beneath his chin. "You've been doing what your father used to do. I suspected as much."

"You know about my father's actual journeys?" The master raised both brows.

"Besides your mother, it was I who knew what your father really did," Decimus replied. "Did you get that bump on your recent, uh, trip?"

The master fingered the bruise on his head. "Yes."

"This is the problem I foresee, Excellency. You wake this morning in strange clothing. You speak about a book, something not known in this time."

"Books are wondrous things, Decimus."

It had been a long time since Decimus heard excitement in his master's voice.

"Imagine many scrolls bound together revealing a marvellous story or filled with facts you could learn." The master sat back in his chair. "I often wonder how my father acquired such a reading instrument, but since I've been to the future, I see books all the time. I even sell them, can you believe it?" A corner of his mouth lifted. "Me, a merchant." He thumbed his chest. "I never thought I'd enjoy doing something like that, but I do.

Decimus looked around. "If I were you, I'd keep that to myself."

"No one knows but you."

"Your problems will multiply if you act like a wild man, a man of *your station*, telling all the world that you've been to the future, where you labour." Decimus shook his head. "And *do not* run through the streets telling everyone you need a woman."

The master's face grew red. Whether it was from embarrassment or anger, Decimus did not know, or care. He had his master's welfare on his mind.

Decimus leant forward and drummed his fingers on the table. "This book, tell me more about it."

"The book's cover I referred to contains a rare gem—"

"Ah, yes. The 'gemma'. Orange, with deep, red hues?"

The master frowned. "You know about that?"

"Your father mined those gems secretly. He claimed he saw strange beings from a faraway placed called a 'distant planet' bury them here underground. The gems held a secret power. You could get to the future, or go backwards in time by stroking those stones in a certain way." Decimus ran a finger around the rim of his goblet. "But your father's mining efforts turned up one rare, orange-coloured gemma. It became very dear to him."

"That's probably why he hid it in the book." Dejection crossed the master's face.

"Are you upset, Excellency?"

"I, uh, no." He shook his head. "Not at all."

He lies, mostly, to himself. "I believe your father feared that someone might take the magic stone from him." Decimus lowered his voice. "You know how your fellow citizens view magic. To them, it is like power, and if you have power and they do not, they feel they must take it from you...by treachery."

The master rubbed his forehead. "Then you see why I must find that book, and the woman. She took the book with her when she fell into the portal."

"And that's when you went after her."

"Yes." He nodded. "She stroked that stone and opened the gateway to the past. I just hope she is not hurt or lost in another time."

"If that book was so important, why did you let her handle it?"

The master's face tightened. Decimus knew he was angry, but reasoned he'd rather see that than devastation on his master's face.

"Because I thought with my loins instead of my head!"

Decimus bit down on his lower lip to stop his grin.

"I see you smiling, Decimus, so just stop." His master's voice held grim notes. His face was serious, while his tone was light. He often did that to cover his true feelings.

Ah, so that's it! It is the woman. She's got him by the balls, and yet, I sense something else.

Decimus nodded. "Go home, Excellency. Wait there. I will make some discreet inquiries. She could very well be here in the city. I will endeavour to find out."

The master rose to his feet and placed a hand on Decimus' shoulder. "Say nothing about the book, or that stone."

"Fear nothing, Excellency."

"Decimus, you have *no* idea how scared I am."

* * * *

Lyla was terrified.

She couldn't feel her wrists anymore. A cold numbness permeated every pore of her body. She forced saliva down her throat, hoping it would quench her thirst.

She had to pee, too.

Tremors racked her body. She shuddered, trying to stem her body's need to relieve itself.

Light from the torches on the walls surrounding her cage brought her surroundings into view.

Her captors sat on the filthy pavement, playing a dice game. Occasionally, one of them would look at her. Sometimes, they'd make crude gestures, like grabbing their cocks and pointing them at her and the other women. Then they'd laugh.

She wanted to die.

One man tossed his dice against a nearby wall and rose to his feet.

He walked over where a young, dark-skinned woman was shackled in the same way as Lyla. He opened the door to the cage and unfastened the woman's hands.

She dropped to the ground and whimpered in pain, rubbing her chafed wrists.

The man yanked her to her feet. Then he fondled her breasts.

The woman stood there, silent, but Lyla saw the tears running down her face.

He called to his companions.

Bile rose in Lyla's throat. She yanked on her chains in an attempt to free herself.

The other men walked over and joined him.

Lyla sucked in a breath and watched, horrified and helpless, while two men turned the woman around and bent her forward. The man with the scar running across his eye stood behind her. He lifted the woman's filthy dress, revealing her naked ass.

He exposed his cock, then pushed it against the woman's backside

"Stop it!" Lyla shouted. She twisted and pulled at the manacles that secured both her hands.

The young woman cried, the sound pitiful.

Crack!

For just a second, Lyla thought she heard a gunshot.

Crack!

That short, beady-eyed man walked in, holding a large whip. Its thin, willowy, metal-tipped lashes landed on the back of the man who had the scar running across his eye.

Odd thoughts filled her mind. She suddenly remembered her conversation with Mark in the bookstore.

"That particular punishment instrument is an early form of a whip known as a flagrum."

"Must've hurt."

"Not as much as the later version. That one had metal tips attached to the lashes..."

She was pulled back to reality when the man yelped in pain, turning blazing eyes on his assaulter, but then he backed away.

The other men soon followed.

The man who held the whip shouted at the other men, his voice booming. He shoved the dark girl back in her cage, shackling her. Her sobs grew broken, her body sagging against the bars.

The man in charge hit the scarred man with the whip's handle. The force of the blow made him reel backwards into a wall.

He cracked the whip again and shouted orders. Then he pointed at Lyla, and spoke rapidly, but she didn't understand a word he said.

A stream of warm water inched down her leg.

The man with the whip watched her wet her shorts, then he laughed, the sound rough and cruel.

He walked over to her cage and reached in through the bars, flicking one of her nipples with his index finger. To make matters worse, he rubbed two fingers between her legs, the damp material of her underwear and shorts scraping against her tender flesh.

She couldn't stop shaking, his touch repugnant, but she'd be damned if she'd do anything else to humiliate herself before this horrible creature. Lyla called on every ounce of strength she possessed to stop her bladder from completely unleashing itself.

He stared at her naked chest, but she refused to cower. He nodded his head, a slow smile spreading across his ugly little face.

She sagged against the bars when he and his men left.

Time crept by.

Lyla didn't know how long she stood shackled to the inside of the cage, her arms high above her head. She took short, shallow breaths, unable to get deep air into her lungs.

She slumped back against the bars despair filling her. Her one thought was if she got away from this terrible place, she'd kill every one of these men, and wouldn't bat an eye doing it.

Chapter Four

Later, the sun dipped further towards the horizon, yet it still blazed as the hour of three rolled around. The atrium was secluded, little used now except for when his Excellency met with dignitaries and other important people. Here, no one would bother him, thinking he had some important, surreptitious meeting. Unlike his less formal courtyard, he could remain here, unbothered by the servants.

Inside the small space, he paced, reminding himself to remain calm, and let Decimus discover what he could. The wily, old servant knew his way around the city and its gossip better than he did.

Time had him on a leash, forcing him to wait for Decimus to return with news.

If Decimus didn't arrive soon, he'd go back to searching for the woman himself, and the consequences be damned! Let his fellow citizens think him mad…

Decimus' voice brought his frenzied walk to a halt. "Master, I have news about the woman."

He strode over to his steward. "What is it?"

"Rumours are rife today."

He sighed, his voice filled with derision. "When *isn't* our grand city *not* filled with hearsay?"

"I've heard that there is to be a special sale today at the Graecostadium."

Blood pounded in his ears. His heart raced.

"One woman is Nubian, the other, a vibrant redhead, and the last is carbasaorum."

"Carbasaorum?" He gripped Decimus' shoulders. "Are you sure the woman has flaxen hair?"

Decimus nodded. "Positive. I've heard she speaks in a strange tongue, also."

He could no longer contain his excitement. Hope sprang, like the waters that rose from the magnificent, tiered fountain they stood next to.

"Excellency, have you considered that this woman may not be the one you search for?"

"If I think that way, then all is lost. Whether or not she is the woman I seek, I would hate to see any woman subjected to Corvus."

Decimus smiled. "You are a good man, Master."

"You are wrong, Decimus." He shook his head. "I am desperate."

* * * *

A few minutes later, Decimus had his conveyance ready and waiting.

He hoisted his tall frame into it then he sat there, drumming his fingers on the padded seat while he waited for Decimus to get in.

The curtains parted. A servant helped Decimus inside. It was a big climb for the elderly little man, his movements slow.

"What took you so long?" he snapped. Each second that went by meant that the woman would slip further away from him. *So would the book.*

Facing the rear of the litter, his body shot forward in the seat when the vehicle moved. Soon, they were on their way to the Graecostadium, travelling at a steady gait.

"I'm sorry I was tardy, Excellency, but I didn't want anyone on the outside to overhear where we're going. I instructed your lead bearers to take another route."

He placed a fisted hand on his thigh, pushing it against the muscles in his leg. Every connective tissue in his body grew taut with resistance. He noticed a strained look on Decimus' face. "Decimus, forgive my outburst. My mind is on the woman."

"As it should be." Decimus angled his head. "We should discuss our strategy."

"What strategy?"

"If Corvus senses even the slightest weakness in you, he'll drive up the price."

"I don't care. I'll pay whatever I have to."

"It could bankrupt you. How would that help this woman?"

Damn, he hated when Decimus was right. "I'll borrow money from my cousin."

Decimus sat forward, a scowl on his face. "Excellency, do you really want your family involved in this? If your cousin knew what you desired, don't you think he'd make trouble? He's always been envious and tries to covet what you have."

"Then what do you suggest?" He raised a brow, realising that Decimus was correct once more.

"The gossip around town is that this flaxen-haired woman speaks a foreign language, like the one you taught me and Appia."

"So?"

Decimus stroked his chin, his face thoughtful. "We could say that we are looking for a tutor for your nephew."

"I don't have any nephews."

"Corvus wouldn't know that. Besides, a woman who speaks a different tongue could be useful as a teacher, or anything else."

He nodded. "An excellent idea."

"It is a sound reason for purchase, as well as not making you appear too vulnerable."

"You never told me who bids against me."

"That we won't know until we get there, but I've requested a private viewing of the woman. You and you alone will see if she is the one you seek."

Hot blood surged to his groin when he thought about being alone with the woman again.

He'd relish every second.

* * * *

Sometime later, one of Lyla's captors came back. He released her wrists from the shackles.

Blood poured into her numb arms and wrists. She cried out in pain while her limbs sprang to life. She wiggled her fingers, hoping the movement would quell the awful feeling of pins and needles running through them.

Now, with her arms at her sides, she could breathe properly again. She took in huge breaths, but the oxygen rush made her head spin.

The man with the jagged scar watched her movements, settling his one good eye on her naked chest.

You dirty son of a bitch. "Like what you see?" Her voice filled with scorn despite her wooziness.

She attempted to pull her shredded clothing over her bare breasts, but he slapped her hands away.

He spat a stream of brown fluid. It hit the floor of her cage. "Meretricis!" he shouted.

She reared back, his spittle splashing her legs. Lyla dearly wished she knew what that word meant. She used her single defence, her mouth. "Bastard," she hissed.

He may not have understood the word, but he did recognise her tone. His face clouded with anger. Then he smiled, revealing his black, rotted teeth.

Let him look his fill. The minute he lets me out of here, I'll scratch out his other eye.

He opened the door to the cage and dragged her out.

She clawed his cheek with her French-manicured nails, catching the corner of his good eye.

Blood dripped down his face.

"Arghhhhhhhhh!" he cried, fingering his injured skin. He grabbed her hair and wrenched her forward, pushing her towards the stairway.

Nausea rolled in her belly. Her legs almost buckled on the steps.

He shoved her inside a small room containing a wooden table. Then he placed a placard around her neck. He got down on his haunches and grabbed her right foot, scraping several chalk lines across the top. Soon, her entire instep was covered in fine, white powder.

Then he left the room.

She stood perfectly still, not daring to move. Her lower lip quivered, but Lyla refused to give it to terror. She walked over to the door that he exited through. When she tried to open it, the damn thing wouldn't budge.

She turned around, noticing an opening in the wall. It was a horizontal slit, big enough to look through. She peered into that opening, her gaze met by a pair of dark eyes. Dark, fine hair lined the person's angular chin, making her realise a man watched her through that opening.

She sucked in a breath, afraid to release it.

Soon, footsteps echoed outside. Lyla turned, her hand going to her throat, where her placard dangled from a crude, rough rope.

The door to the room slid open.

For a few seconds, she just stood there, not sure what to do. Then her eyes widened as recognition dawned.

"Oh, my God!" She placed her palm against her mouth, but her hand shook uncontrollably.

In the next instant, she had her arms around the man's neck.

"I'm so g-glad it's you." She couldn't stop blubbering. "I d-didn't think I'd see you again."

The man didn't release her at first. He stood there quietly, allowing her to cry.

She moved her face from his shoulder then his eyes met hers once more. She pounded his chest with her fists. "Where have you been?"

He stilled her movements, grasping her wrists in his large hands, and she cried out in pain. He looked down at her scraped, bruised flesh. "I could kill Corvus for doing this to you." He spoke in English, his voice low and menacing.

He examined each wrist, holding them in the palm of one hand, stroking the fingers of his other hand across her chafed, raw, skin.

His touch was electrifying, sending shockwaves of need through her body. Tears pooled in her eyes. His caress was the first gentle, kind act she experienced since she arrived in this strange, terrible place.

"Wh-who is this Corvus person?"

The man shook his head. "You don't know?"

"How *would* I?"

"Corvus accepted my bid."

"Your—*bid*? For what?"

"You."

She froze. "Do you mean to tell me, I'm for sale, and this Corvus is doing the selling?"

"That is correct."

Her mouth hung open.

"Do as I say, Lyla," he bent and whispered in her ear, "and you'll leave here alive with me, but from now on, you will address me as Master."

Her chest heaved, despite her relief at being rescued. "Like that's likely to happen."

"Don't push me to do something I don't want to, Lyla."

Her name, uttered in his deep voice made her want to cry all over again. "*Your name* is Mark Hardin, but I should address you as 'Master'?"

His face tightened, but she pushed on. "You own that bookstore. Or was that all bullshit?" She trembled. "Now, you're here to bid on me, which means, you're going to *buy me*. Is that correct?" She lifted her chin, it quivered, despite her show of bravado. "I'm not for sale."

He spoke through clenched teeth. "*Here* you will address me properly. It will be Master." He grasped her shoulders between his large hands. "And you have no say in what is about to happen. We are being watched," he murmured, nodding towards the opening in the wall.

Lyla noticed the scene before her. Several men stood on the other side of that viewer, their gazes locked with hers.

"I have paid much for you, but Corvus would seal the bargain and give you to me only if I allowed him and his cohorts to watch my inspection of your body. A body," his voice dipped, "which he has assured me is ripe and luscious." His eyes sought her bared breasts.

"Go to hell." She clenched her jaw. Her hands fisted by her sides. "I won't let you do that to me." What she wouldn't give to take a swing at him!

He stepped behind her, running his hands over her shoulders. "I will give you back to Corvus if you continue to defy me. It will not go well for you."

The thought of them putting their hands on her again sent shivers down her spine.

"Strip," he commanded, his deep voice settling in the juncture between her thighs.

"N-no." Her voice wobbled. "I won't." She moved away from him.

He folded his arms across his chest. Here in this small room he looked tough and commanding, his tall frame filling the space. His sun-kissed, olive-toned skin stood out against the stark white colour of the long tunic he wore. A red cloak swathed his body, held in place by a brooch at his shoulder.

"Strip, or I will do it for you. It is your choice." His commanding tone brooked no argument.

Lyla thought quickly. If she didn't do as he said, he'd give her to those men behind the peephole.

She discarded her shredded bra and tank top then unbuttoned her shorts. She whisked them and her hip-hugging panties down her thighs. She tossed them at Mark and he caught them deftly in one large hand.

The men behind the wall laughed.

Lyla stood there, wearing nothing but her nakedness. Her ears buzzed, but she willed herself to remain upright.

Mark grasped her shoulders gently, turning her so that she faced him. His tender touch on her shoulders made her vulnerable. Had her mind become so twisted, was she so insane, that she sought to bond with him in some crazy way? A strange feeling of anticipation filled her. Perhaps her mind had folded, and she'd gone insane, but God help her, she wanted to preen before him...

He glanced at her foot marked with the chalk and nodded. "Ah, so you are new, my sweet. That is good." He cocked his head. "Then again, I must be sure."

A shuddering sob escaped her.

"I won't hurt you." He lowered his voice, the deep timber soothing. "But you must trust me. If you struggle, I'll be forced to give these men the show they expect."

He stroked her hair. *"Is gero haud pillai."* He spoke in that strange language, directing his comment towards the other side of the wall. His mouth lifted, aiming his next comment in English, at her. "If you wear no cap, then it means Corvus guarantees you are special. I would like to see just how unique you are."

Her eyes widened.

Again, he addressed the men behind the wall. *"Tamen ego must exsisto certus."*

She heard the men snort and laugh.

"I have to examine you." He spoke again in a low, soothing tone. "If I don't, Corvus won't think my bid is legitimate."

A sick, sinking feeling landed in the pit of her belly.

"Just stand still. I won't hurt you, but it must be done." He ran a finger down her arm.

She shuddered, but not from cold. The heat from his touch made her flesh burn. Her shuddering turned violent.

The men behind the wall laughed again, then they cheered, speaking in their strange tongue, their voices raised high.

"Ignore them," Mark told her. "Focus on something else."

She didn't dare look at him, choosing to stare at a spot on the wall behind him.

The minute he stroked her breasts, she almost fell to her knees. The smooth pads of his fingers glided across her nipples. They pebbled into hard little buds. His touch travelled clear down to her pussy, despite her efforts to fight it.

Mark ran his fingers down her back. He stroked her bottom cheeks, lifting them in his hands, sliding his thumbs up, then down her flesh.

She heard the men's rumbling laughter and their crude tone, even if she didn't understand what they said.

Mark whispered in her ear, his voice raspy, "If I could, I would kill them all." His warm breath circled her lobe. "I would be alone with you and do this, like I've dreamt of doing ever since I met you."

Her knees almost buckled, but he held a firm grip beneath her elbows.

His hands returned to her backside. She sucked in a breath when his finger skimmed the cleft between her ass cheeks.

He spoke in a hushed tone. "This is expected. If I don't do this, they will think something is amiss." He stroked her bottom again. "I won't penetrate you, but I need you to cry," he whispered. "That way, they will think I have punctured your *solum*."

He slid his finger down the cleft between her butt cheeks.

She whimpered, not because he caused her pain, but because his touch made her feel so damned good.

The men laughed and continued to watch through the viewer.

Mark left his index finger there, placing the tip of it against the space between her ass cheeks, but he kept his promise and didn't push it inside. Then he shouted something in that foreign tongue.

Lyla heard more snickers from the men.

He ran his thumb along her jaw. "This will soon be over."

She could fight him, and give them a show they'd expect, but that would cause her more pain or even death. The will to survive grew in her like a giant tidal wave. It crashed over her, and when it receded, she realised it had filled her with inner strength.

He led her to a table. Then he placed his hands around Lyla's waist and lifted her, her bottom contacting with the rough wood.

"Lay back," he commanded. "Spread your legs."

He was mad, to tell her to do such a thing. Tears filled her eyes. She couldn't stem their flow. She wiped them away, listening while the men jeered. Tunnelling deep within herself, she pulled out all her reserves.

Back in that bookstore, she had wanted to know what Mark's touch would feel like. *Be careful what you wish for...*

"Ego sum iens ut inspect suus vallum!" Mark said, loud enough for the men outside the viewing room to hear.

Vallum. She comprehended that word, damn it. He would inspect her pussy, and those men would see him do it.

She knew Mark's gentle touch now, but she couldn't trust what he'd do if she fought him. A tiny part of her didn't want to. Shame washed over her. Her emotions careened wildly. Anger, humiliation, and desire warred with each other.

She settled her body on the table, the wood scraping her back. All she could see was the ceiling.

"Open your legs."

She hesitated for just a minute, then lifted them onto the table, spreading them wide.

He placed his palm against her pussy. His open hand brushed the curls there, tickling her. He massaged her clit, running the pad of his middle finger against it.

She sucked in a breath, her orgasm building, surprised that he could arouse her to passion, despite her precarious circumstances. In her mind, she fought the feeling, guilt mingling with her desire. How could she feel such exquisite sensations? She should be fighting him.

But the more he rubbed, the wetter she became. Her back arched, her nails digging into the wood. Then he pulled his hand away before she came. Her frustrated cry made the men laugh again.

Tears filled her eyes. They spilled over, landing on her cheeks.

Mark lifted her from the table, setting her on her feet. He removed the large, red cape-like material from his shoulders and swirled it around hers. It settled across her body, his exotic, unique smell captured in the soft cloth.

Lyla had trouble concentrating. Everything took on a surreal quality. She slipped peacefully into madness, where no one and nothing could hurt her.

No! Her mind clashed against the feeling, knowing that if she gave in, she'd be lost forever.

She had to fight—even if her only ammunition was her words. She told herself to struggle, to continue the battle against the danger around her. Persistence and perseverance would be her weapons.

Mark hustled her from the small room and down a narrow corridor. Outside, he brought her to a litter attended by several men. She stopped dead in her tracks.

Who travelled like this?

Once, she rode in a small carriage drawn by a man on the boardwalk in Atlantic City, New Jersey. It had been novel at the time, and saved her from walking the boardwalk's vast length.

Now, gazing at the men shackled to the vehicle before her, shame washed over her when she recalled that ride in that litter on Atlantic City's boardwalk. These men who stood chained to this litter looked tired and haggard, their heads bent, their bodies sagging. The hot sun beat down upon their heads. Perspiration tracks lined their broad backs. It flowed down their skin in large rivulets, making their wide backs shiny.

She glanced to her left, then to her right, looking for the perfect opportunity to make a run for it.

"Don't." Mark had a firm grip on her upper arm. "Runaway slaves must live like fugitives. They're always caught...and killed."

She rounded on him. "I'm a slave?"

"Precisely."

Anxiety filled her gut. Her stomach ached with it. If she got inside that litter, she didn't know what would happen to her or if she'd ever be heard from again.

"It is your choice, Lyla. Run away, and my men will hunt you down and bring you back. Your punishment will be severe." He nodded towards the vehicle. "You decide. Punishment, or a comfortable ride home, where I can attend to your wounds."

*How strange...*he spoke of home like she should remember it, as though she resided there with him. Or perhaps he just messed with her mind as a way to draw her into his confidence.

Yeah, she had gone insane. But she still had a brain to help her decide.

If she ran now, exhaustion and hunger would overtake her. She wanted to live. And she still had an ounce of fight left... "I'll go with you, but only if you promise to release those other women."

He raised a brow. "What other women?"

"In the two cages across from mine. One is dark-skinned, the other a redhead."

He scowled. "I do not make deals with slaves."

"Please help them." She laid a hand on his arm. When he raised one dark brow and looked down at her hand, she removed it. "You rescued me from that awful place, can't you find it in your heart to help them?"

"Decimus!" he shouted.

Seconds later, a little old man walked up to him.

The elderly man cast her a furtive glance, his frown deepening the more he and Marcus spoke in their odd language. Then Decimus stalked away, entering the area she and Mark had recently exited.

"It shall be done. The women will be released," Mark stated.

"How do I know you'll do what you said?"

"You don't. All you have my word, but my word is sacred." He sighed. "Will you *please* get in the litter now?"

Please? His courtesy threw her off balance. If she heard him correctly, it almost sounded like he begged her to get in. "You swear to me that you're going to help those women?"

He stepped closer. "I never break a promise." His deep, low tone vibrated with suppressed anger, and something else. Lyla thought he sounded...disappointed. "Did I keep my word to you while we were in that room?"

He had her there. While what he did had been degrading, he did it quickly and gently. Then again, some kinky edge to her personality, liked it.

"My actions allowed you to live. Never forget that."

Lyla swayed on her feet, the day's gruesome events catching up with her, the truth of his statement making her realise, she was now *his* prisoner.

Before she could utter any protest, Mark lifted her in his arms and placed her in the litter. Her bottom connected with a padded seat.

She scooted into the corner, shoving her aching body as far into the small space as possible.

Mark got in after her. He leaned out the opening and shouted something to his men.

Soon the litter moved.

Lyla wondered how long it would be before someone back home would miss her—maybe someone at BestUCanBe. Then again, they might think that she had decided to stay a few more days in Cape Cod. If that were the case, she'd have no job when she got back.

If she got away from this hellhole.

She hadn't heard from her parents in ages, and if she were honest, she'd say that she, and them, had fallen into a comfortable incommunicado.

It suddenly occurred to her... No one would give a rat's ass about Lyla Thomas.

Chapter Five

Lyla stayed huddled in the corner, near the headrest. Her mind filled with escape plans, despite Mark's threat of punishment.

She had to try. Otherwise, how could she live with herself?

She glanced through the slit in the curtains. If she could just engage Mark in conversation, if she could *distract* him... An idea bloomed.

Lyla couldn't imagine what he planned for her once they arrived at their destination — wherever that was. It could be worse than that man Corvus' dungeon-like place.

If she tried to escape, Mark might punish her with torture until she cried out for death's release. Maybe his gentleness was all a façade, a way to draw her into his trust then he'd make her *wish* for her life to end. Then again, once they got to their destination, Mark might just torture her anyway.

Or would he? She couldn't be sure of anything in this crazy place!

No matter which scenario she chose, she felt well and truly fucked. She made her decision.

Running her tongue over her lips, she hoped to make them wet and shiny, but she was so damned thirsty it seemed almost impossible to get any saliva into her mouth.

She sat up and tossed back her hair, hoping she appeared bold. Sliding a corner of the red cape down her shoulders, she revealed one bare breast, just enough so that it would get his attention.

Mark's eyes travelled down her body and back up again, settling on her mouth. Then they dropped to her chest, where they stayed.

His bold perusal sent hot, jittery shivers down her spine. They settled in the cleft above her ass then travelled to her pussy where her clit throbbed. *I'm supposed to be turning him on, not the other way around, damn it.*

He stretched out his long legs, resting his head against the padded interior. "You have nothing to fear. I never force myself on a woman."

Fucking bastard! You're a liar. You buy women for your pleasure… You're probably a white-slaver. Someone who purchases women all the time. You're probably going to sell me to someone else for a higher price. I've heard stories about what they do to white women like me.

She couldn't allow fear to control her. She needed to concentrate and play her role as seductress in this macabre situation.

"I know you want me." She kept her voice low and sexy.

His eyes remained on her. "We'll discuss my desire for you later."

Her face heated, but at least she knew he wanted her. This would make everything easier.

"Right now, I must acquire some information."

"What?"

"Where's the book?"

"Book?" She snapped her brows together in thought. Then her eyes widened. She flushed, remembering how fascinated she'd become with that old tome filled with sex drawings. Her preoccupation with that stupid book, and *him*, was what got her in all this trouble. Had she been paying attention, she would have been wise to his tricks.

She couldn't remember him doing *anything* to her in that bookstore to make her wind up here in this horrible place.

Except his offer to take her to dinner. Had she taken him up on his invite to dine with him?

Maybe he'd drugged her, but...when? She didn't remember being with him in any other place but that bookstore.

"Are we talking about that book filled with porn?"

He pursed his lips together. It appeared as though he did it to keep from laughing. "We are." He angled his head. "Does Corvus have it?"

She truly had absolutely no idea what in hell had happened to that volume filled with ancient pornography.

Mark leant forward. "Does Corvus have the book?"

She shrugged.

"Lyla." Mark's tone deepened. "Do *not* toy with me."

She thought quickly. "It's worth a fortune, that's what Corvus told me." She hoped she could play this out. She sensed desperation in Mark about that book. He obviously wanted it badly...maybe he would go back and get it. *And when they turn this litter around, I can jump out and escape!*

Mark beetled his dark brows. For one crazy, stupid second, she wanted to reach out and soothe his frown.

Concentrate! Focus...don't let that handsome face sway you. She looked down at his calves bulging with muscle. His long, narrow feet did strange things to her insides.

A corner of his mouth lifted. "It won't work."

"What won't?"

"You're lying about that book." A slight movement, like a muscle jumping, belied the anger in his face.

"I'm not lying."

"Then tell me who Corvus is."

Think! Think! "He's, uh, the uh, man who sold me to you."

He snorted. "Nice try."

"Well, he is, isn't he?"

"What does he look like?"

Her brain leapt into action. "He looks small and like, well, a snake. And he carries a whip."

Mark narrowed his eyes. "I still think you're not telling me the truth."

"Well, I am, about Corvus, and how do you know that I'm not sincere about that book? Go back and question Corvus if you doubt my story."

He pursed his lips, his sensual mouth drawn into a thin line.

Lyla placed her right hand behind her back, crossing her middle and index fingers. She needed all the luck she could get.

"Everything you had with you now belongs to me. If Corvus took your possessions, and didn't surrender them, he will pay for it with his life," Mark said through clenched teeth. He shouted something out the window to his men in that foreign language. "Subsisto!"

She hoisted her body from the seat. Pain shot through her wrists and hands, making it hard to grasp anything. Ignoring it, she tried again, her head peeking through the curtains.

Now, if she could just muster the strength to push herself from the litter...

She caught a glimpse of the ground below. It whizzed by at breakneck speed, the drop to the pavement farther than she thought. *I can do this! I can...*

The litter came to a sudden stop, jerking her body backwards, loosening her grasp.

A steely arm wrapped around her waist.

"Ow!" she cried, when the back of her head hit something sharp and pointy.

"Damn you!" Mark's shout echoed through the confined space.

She glanced back to see him rub his jaw, in that exact spot where she must have connected with it.

"Have you lost your mind?" he shouted.

She was trapped between his legs. She pushed and shoved at the hard arm locked around her waist. "Let me go!" She hoped someone passing by would hear. Maybe they'd summon help.

Mark leaned his head out the opening and called to his men, but he didn't release her. Her body jolted forward then back when the litter swayed and picked up speed.

Mark kept a firm grip on her and growled low in her ear. "How could you be that stupid to try and jump from a moving litter?"

She grumbled, annoyed that her plan failed. "I wanted to do it when it stopped." She lifted her chin, tears stinging her eyes as disappointment and humiliation filled her. "I'd rather die than stay with you, because you're going to sell me."

He released her. She dove for the corner. Tears threatened to spill from her eyes but she'd be damned if she'd cry in full view of Mark.

"I'm not going to sell you to anyone."

"You're a white slaver, aren't you?"

"Far from it." He ran a hand through his dark, wavy hair, his face filled with the same frustrated look.

She wouldn't cry, damn it! She wouldn't...

"Come here, Lyla." His voice held soft, tender notes.

"No." She sniffed back a sob. It caught in her throat, almost choking her.

"You must learn to do as I command. It will be much easier if you do."

She swiped at her runny nose. "I'll *never* obey you."

"You're very brave," he replied. "But very, very foolish." He reached for her.

She slapped his hands away, but he was stronger. He didn't release her, lifting her as though she weighed no more than a bag of feathers. Her bottom met his hard, muscular thighs. He wrapped his arms around her, holding her close.

She sucked in a breath, his warm, caring touch making her want to break down and weep. She fought the urge to cuddle against him.

One minute, he was dominant and commanding, and the next, he showed her the most exquisite gentleness. She didn't know what to think anymore.

"I will not hurt you," he told her.

Lyla struggled in his embrace, but the more she did, the tighter his hold became. She became cocooned in his arms, yet he did as he promised and didn't harm her, just held her in place, until she ceased her movements.

Tears spilled from her eyes. They dripped down her face, wetting her cheeks and chin. He leant down and sipped at them, capturing her face between his large, warm hands.

Lyla clung to him, his delightful scent filling her nose.

He cupped the back of her head, bringing her face down to his shoulder. She wept loudly, her hands grasping his clothing. Pushing her fists into his chest, she cried until she hadn't a tear left in her eyes. Then her sobs quieted.

"Better?" he murmured, stroking her head. His hand slipped lower, to her back. He traced circles there with his palm.

She released a sigh. It came from deep within her. Then she lifted her face from his shoulder and gazed into his eyes. They weren't hard or cruel; they looked like dark, smouldering embers.

Desire, swift and sure hit her full force. Her pussy throbbed. The tip of his hard cock rubbed against her clit. Her breasts grew heavy.

He slipped the red cape lower, until her upper body was fully exposed.

"Rub your little bud against my cock."

"And if I don't?" She raised a brow. Her heart raced despite her boldness.

She also knew it beat in double time because she wanted to do just what he commanded.

"I would hate to have to chastise you after the ordeal you've been through." He ran a finger down her breast. "Your choice. Punishment, or making love with me here, now."

Lyla bristled. "Go ahead, beat me. That's the only way I'll allow you to touch me."

"You'd rather have a beating? My men outside would hear your screams. Is that what you want?"

"You're insane." She trembled at the thought. "Why would I want that?"

She remembered the mean-looking whip Corvus used on his men...and her. While Mark possessed no lash, he had large hands. She'd never survive a blow from him.

Beatings in this godforsaken, horrible place seemed to be an everyday happening.

"It must make you feel like a real man to pummel someone half your size." She aimed her chin at him at a defiant angle.

He blinked once, confusion lining his face.

"I'd fight you with every ounce of strength I had in me." Her voice broke on a sob. She covered her mouth with her hand.

"You think I intend to—" He scrubbed a hand over his face. In the next instant, he pushed her from his lap. "I will not bother you again."

Bother me? Now she swore she heard things.

When his eyes met hers, it seemed as though it took a great force of will to look at her. "I will not touch you."

"You're trying to trick me, is that it?"

"Absolutely not." A muscle in his jaw moved.

"So now, you don't want to make love with me?"

His eyes flew to hers. "I didn't say that. But I also don't force myself on women who aren't willing." He scowled. "And I do *not* pummel them."

Memories of his hands caressing her body in that viewing room made her clit throb. She shifted on the seat to quell the sweet ache blooming inside her. Her emotions didn't make sense to her anymore.

"You certainly didn't mind *bothering me* before."

"You must understand that if I didn't examine you, Corvus would have never sold you to me."

He had trouble meeting her gaze. If she didn't know better, she might believe he actually seemed disturbed about what he did to her in that viewing room.

"Corvus would have killed you if I didn't."

She wanted to cry all over again. This had to be the craziest thing she'd ever contemplated, but damn, she wanted to be back on his lap. Despite anything else she might think, she had to admit that he hadn't invaded her body or hurt her, and almost brought her to orgasm.

Truth be told, it had filled her with lust to not cower in front of those men. Power fuelled her desire.

She'd be damned if she'd accept Mark's rejection now. Looking down at his lap, she noticed something rise to the occasion. She got up from her seat and settled on his thighs, easing her bottom down on the hard leg muscles.

"What are you doing?" He snapped his brows together.

"What does it look like?"

He grabbed her shoulders between his hands. "Stop. Now."

"No."

"You've just been through a very stressful situation. You don't know what you're doing."

"Yeah, well, let's just call this *stress relief.*"

Her hands grasped his tunic. She pushed it up until his penis jutted out. God, he was big! She licked her lips.

His eyes lit with need. They resembled deep, dark, coffee.

She had to be mad to even *consider* doing this…

She shimmied closer, her hands on his shoulders. Then she placed her naked clit against his penis. She rubbed herself against him, his cock's rigid contours skimming her little pleasure button.

He didn't move; he let her do the work.

A trembling feeling, more forceful than any vibrator, pulsed against her.

"My men are carrying the litter across a particularly rough patch of pavement," Marcus whispered near her ear. "Their quick footsteps over the uneven stones make the litter shake."

"Oh...*my*." Her eyes widened while her orgasm grew. Her pussy throbbed, its beat matching the litter's rhythm while it moved.

"It will give you much satisfaction," he murmured. Then he dipped his tongue inside her ear.

She trembled with delight when he blew against her lobe.

"*My* pleasure will always be to give you pleasure, Lyla, no matter what you desire."

He kissed her, holding her face between his hands, his tongue sliding across her lips. He pressed the tip of his tongue against her mouth, coaxing it open. Her mouth parted, and so did something inside her. A wellspring filled with fear, need, and pleasure burst forth.

She clutched his shoulders while she came, her wet pussy drenching his cock with her cum.

Her body folded against him, while a shudder tore through his. He trembled against her. She heard the racing beat of his heart.

She waited, expecting him to do more, to force her into submission. She had to be a complete lunatic to initiate this. Instead, he sat still, holding her against his chest.

Then he covered her with that red cape, shifting so that he could tug his clothing down.

She stayed on his lap her mind and body drained. Her eyes became heavy. She couldn't keep them open.

Soon, she slumped against him and settled into a dreamless slumber.

* * * *

Much later, Lyla's eyelids fluttered open. She squinted against the bright sun that shone through a lone window.

When she could focus, she noticed she lay on a bed in a small room that contained a table, a chair, and nothing else. She glanced upwards at a small window. No glass pane covered it. No curtain blew in the breeze. The opening was small and as bare as the sparse furnishings.

She heard sounds outside. Men, women and children spoke in some odd language, the cadence and pitch of their voices something Lyla thought she *should* know, but couldn't comprehend. Footsteps echoed on the pavement, mingling with the sounds of horses and other animals. A bird's shrill cry filled her ears. Then it disappeared.

She waited, hoping to hear some traffic noise. Somewhere in the distance, a horn trumpeted.

Her shoulders slumped when she realised it was not a car horn blast, but an animal's call. Perhaps it was an elephant...

Sweat trickled down her chest. The hot weather made her think Mark held her captive in the Middle East, but the foreign tongue everyone spoke didn't sound Arabic.

Then again, it could be some elaborate ploy to confuse her. She didn't know what to think anymore.

Just as she slid her legs from the bed, a door slid open.

She held her breath, her eyes seeking something she could grab to throw at the intruder.

A young woman stuck her head inside the room. She spoke in halting English. "You're awake." She nodded. "My master was starting to worry."

"Who is your master?" Lyla ventured to ask.

The girl's face split into a wide grin. "His Excellency, Marcus Fla—"

"Marcus," Lyla repeated. She narrowed her eyes. "You mean, Mark Hardin, don't you?"

The young woman angled her head, her face thoughtful. "I know no one by that name, but *my* master is his Excellency, Marcus Flavius Valerius."

Lyla glanced at the open door. If she could just tip that basket the girl held between her hands and create a diversion...

The aroma of warm bread drifted by her nose. It made her stomach rumble. Okay, so she'd make her escape *after* she ate.

The basket contained bread and an assortment of fruits and cheese. She sniffed the air, a delicious, tangy scent filling her senses, as well as something that smelt like a roasted pepper.

When she glanced at the basket again, she noticed a small container filled with plump, little red peppers, nestled in red sauce. She wondered if they were as hot as they appeared, for they were like the tiny, spicy cherry peppers she purchased in a jar back home.

The attention to detail, to what she liked, made her wary. How did this girl know she liked spicy food? Had Mark told her?

"My master said you'd probably be hungry, but if I brought you that stuffed dormouse like I did to him yesterday he'd..." The girl stopped talking, and placed the basket on a table near the bed, but not before Lyla noticed the high colour in the young woman's cheeks.

Lyla ripped a piece of the warm, rustic-looking bread from a loaf. She chewed and swallowed, closing her eyes, savouring the flavour. It was soft on the inside, crusty on the outside.

She reached for a grape, its juicy goodness sliding down her parched throat.

The young girl poured some liquid into a cup that resembled and smelt like wine.

Lyla just looked at it.

"Go on," the girl told her. "Drink it. You must be thirsty."

Right. Sure. Maybe it's drugged! Lyla continued to stare at it, biting down hard on her lower lip. But the more she looked at it, the thirstier she became.

Dehydration overshadowed doubt. She sipped the liquid at first. It tasted like sour grape juice, with a few sweet undertones.

"I gave you the watered down wine, I thought the other would go right to your head, after what you've been through."

"You know what happened to me?" Lyla took another draught of the wine.

The girl angled her head. "Of course, I do." She looked at Lyla's hands. "Do your wrists feel better?"

Lyla noticed that the redness, bruising and swelling seemed to have faded somewhat.

"They do feel better," she murmured.

"How about that cut?"

Lyla lifted her arm, noticing a small strip of clean linen covering the nasty wound Corvus inflicted with his lash.

"That seems fine."

"My master tended to your wounds himself."

"He did?" She coughed when a piece of bread lodged in her throat. The girl patted her back and handed her the cup. Lyla gulped down the tangy drink, loosening the dry bread in her throat.

The girl smiled. "My master always does what he promises."

This man, Mark...Marcus...or whatever everyone deemed to call him, seemed an odd mix. His kindness kept her off balance, making her forget his dominant nature and his inspection of her body in Corvus' prison.

Her face heated when she thought about how much she enjoyed his touch, and their lovemaking in his litter. Perhaps her body also responded to his kindness, for he had rescued her, after all.

Lyla tipped her head to one side, suddenly curious about the young woman. "How come you got so embarrassed before?" She reached for some cheese, enjoying its gooey, runny goodness and salty flavour.

She hoped the young girl wouldn't tell her that Mark examined her in the same way he did Lyla. She feared for this girl, but if she were honest, the little twinge of jealousy nipping at her heart is what bothered her more.

The young woman placed her hand over hers. "Here. Allow me. It is better if you spread the cheese on the bread." She did so and placed the bread in Lyla's hand.

She wolfed it down, following it with several sips of wine.

"My master said I could not give you the stuffed dormouse, or he'd beat me."

The hairs on the back of Lyla's neck rose. "He beats you if you disobey?"

The girl nodded, her face colouring again.

Oh, boy.

"I had trouble sitting the last time he did," the young girl murmured.

Lyla thought she might have misunderstood. If she heard the young woman correctly, it actually sounded like this girl's master spanked her.

Her pussy throbbed.

An image popped into her mind of her own body draped over Mark's hard thighs. It made her heart race. She had to think about something else to blot out her erotic thoughts.

Maybe she could pump this girl for information, and use it to aide her escape from this wretched place. Although, when she glanced around the room, she determined that it wasn't so terrible. In fact, it appeared rather pleasant, even if the furnishings were sparse.

No! She couldn't be taken in by her surroundings. Mark probably planned it all to make it *seem* better, when in reality she was nothing more than his prisoner, like she had been with that man Corvus.

She had just traded up, but not for freedom.

"What did you do to earn such a punishment?" Lyla asked, hoping to distract the girl. She glanced at the door, calculating the exact time she could run through it...

"I was very young when I came here—eighteen."

Thoughts of escape flew from her brain. "You were only eighteen?" Lyla's eyes widened.

The girl pushed some long, brown hair behind one ear. "Yes. I was not happy, either."

"I can imagine," Lyla replied, deciding to munch on a grape, curiosity winning over her need to escape in that minute.

"My master had rescued me from a very evil man."

"Who?"

"Corvus. He is a vile, hateful creature. He sells women into prostitution."

Lyla's brow went up. "And this Marcus person got you away from him?"

"Yes."

"But you are still a prisoner. Here. In Marcus' house."

The young girl shook her head. "I'm not. I am his servant."

"Not much difference." Lyla snorted.

The young girl's eyes widened. "Oh, but there is!" She sat down on the bed next to Lyla. "My master has tutored me in many different things." Her smile grew wide. "He is teaching me languages because he feels I am very smart."

"You speak English rather well."

The girl nodded. "My master said that I and Decimus were worth teaching this Eeeenglish to. He also says that knowledge separates us from our fellow men. If I can learn how to behave like a noble woman then everyone will believe I am. And with his backing, I can be a great man's wife some day." She nodded.

Lyla rolled her eyes. "A great thing to aspire to."

"Aspire? What does that mean?"

Lyla batted the air with her hand. "Forget it. So tell me, how did you earn your punishment that time?"

"I missed my family very much. I am from Greece. I wanted to go back to them."

"Understandable." Lyla nodded.

"Yes, but I had to realise that I would never see them again, and that my master's home would be mine, as well. I ran away, determined not to accept what had happened to me. I made it from the house and into the street. A platoon of soldiers headed right towards me. They stop for nothing and no one. I-I would have been trampled."

"Someone rescued you?"

"The master." The young girl sighed. "And punished me swiftly. I have never forgotten it." She shifted on the bed, lifting one butt cheek, then the other. Her face grew pink. "He told me I had placed myself in great danger, and for that, I had to be chastised."

Lyla's bottom tingled. She wondered if her face seemed as red as the girl's. Her cunt was damp, too. *Stupid. Why am I reacting this way?*

How strange, I would have thought he'd kill her. Instead, he spanks her for putting her life in jeopardy.

"What's your name?" popped from Lyla's mouth.

"Appia."

"That's lovely."

Appia rose from the bed. Lyla grabbed her hands and placed them in her own.

"Don't let him sell you to another man. Fight it. Fight *him,*" Lyla said through clenched teeth.

"I don't understand."

"You're young, but old enough to decide for yourself. Don't allow your master to give you to another man. You can make your own choices."

"Wh-what do you mean? How can I possibly choose?"

"You're allowing your master to give you to someone you don't know. What if this other man hurts you or —"

"I trust my master. His friend is interested in me. Any true ally of my master will take care of me."

Lyla sighed. "Don't fall for it."

For just a second, the girl looked like she considered her words.

The perfect opportunity surfaced for Lyla to voice her other idea. She lowered her voice. "Appia, how about you and I escape this horrid place together? You could see your family again."

Appia's eyes widened. "You're not serious?"

"I am."

Lyla glanced upwards, at the window. "Give me a leg up."

"A what?"

"Cup your hands together, like this." Lyla turned her hands palm up then laced her fingers together. "You'll be making a kind of step for me. I'll use it to hoist myself through the window."

Appia shook her head. "That window is too small."

"Nonsense. It'll be fine."

"Mistress, this is not a good idea."

"Fine, if you're not going to help me, I'll find some other way," Lyla huffed. She looked around the small room, deciding to move the bed closer to the wall.

"Now what are you doing?" Appia angled her head.

Lyla stood on the bed and placed her hands on the window ledge. She hoisted herself up, hanging onto the sill and poked her head through the opening. Outside on the crowded street, she saw men, women, and children all dressed in odd tunics and capes. They strode along like they didn't have a care in the world.

How she envied them.

She gripped the ledge tighter. Soon, half her body draped over the windowsill. She looked down and dizziness washed over her.

She was two stories up!

"Mistress, please come down."

She wanted to. No way in hell she could jump into the street without breaking her leg, or neck or...

She tried to slide her body backwards but soon realised she couldn't nudge her hips through the opening. Again, she attempted to push herself backwards. "Appia, p-pull on my legs."

The girl tugged on her ankles.

"Ow!" Lyla grimaced. "Not so hard."

"Mistress, you're going to get hurt. I think this escape is—"

"Not happening," came the sound of a deep, male voice.

Lyla cringed when she heard Mark.

"Appia, you may leave," he commanded the young woman.

Shit!

She heard Appia's departing footsteps.

Lyla wiggled her hips, hoping to dislodge them from the tight space.

"Very nice," Mark intoned, patting her ass. A chuckle followed.

Her face heated. Sweat popped out on her forehead. It dripped down her face.

Mark's hands lingered on her tunic. Soon, he pushed it up, trailing his fingers along her skin. He grabbed her calves. "I should really let you stay up there."

"Fine! Go ahead." Embarrassment crashed over her in simmering waves.

"Have it your way."

Her eyes widened when she heard his footsteps.

"Don't leave me up here!" She glanced down at the street. Her head spun.

"Then ask me nicely."

"Please, get me down," she said through clenched teeth.

He tugged on her calves, giving them a hard pull. Her hips finally slid through the narrow opening.

"Ow!" she cried as her body scraped the sides.

Mark caught her around the waist and eased her down on the bed.

She collapsed onto it, rubbing her right hip then her left one.

"Let me see." He started to hike up her tunic.

She slapped his hand away.

He raised a brow. "You had no trouble baring yourself to me in the litter."

"Th-that was different."

"Really?" He rose to his full height and crossed his arms over his chest. "How so?" His mouth lifted in a wry grin.

"Go on." Tears filled her eyes. "Make fun of me. What do I care?"

He raised her chin with the tip of his index finger. "I am not making sport of you, Lyla."

She pushed his finger away. "What happened in the litter..."

"Make no excuse for your desire," he murmured. "I enjoyed it, and I know you did, too. There was no harm in relieving your, um, distress."

"My *distress* is just beginning." She'd enjoyed what happened in the litter far more than what she cared to admit. To him. She still didn't trust him totally.

"While I would love to argue with you, this morning's incident will *not* be debated." He scowled. "Foolish woman, even if you made it through that small window you would have broken your neck on the pavement below. What were you thinking?"

"I guess I wasn't. Thinking, that is."

"Desperation makes people do stupid things. I would hope that you could learn to trust me and —"

She bounded from the bed. "Trust you?" she ground out. "Why should I trust you?"

"Because right now, I'm your only friend."

"Some friend," she muttered. "You bought me, then —"

"Should I have allowed you to languish in Corvus' prison? Or maybe, I should have let some other man, someone who doesn't possess *my* patience, buy you?"

"Now I'm in *your* prison."

"Correction. You are in my *home*. That is a far cry from prison."

"Your home. Prison. What does it matter?" she retorted. "You're still the warden."

"However you wish to view me is your choice."

"Hah!" She slashed a hand before her. "You told me I have to obey you, therefore, I have no say or choice."

"Let me put it to you this way. If you continue to try to escape, I will take you in hand. *That* you have no say in."

She balled her hand into a fist at her side.

He glanced at her hand. "Don't." He shook his head. "It will go badly for you if you hit me."

She hated that he saw through her so easily. "I guess you'll punish me the same way you do your other slaves." She lifted her chin defiantly, but her face burned just the same. Thinking about him spanking that young girl, of him doing the same thing to *her*, made her pussy beat in time with her racing pulse.

He cocked his head, studying her. "You seem to be very interested in punishment."

"Not in the least," she lied.

"Uh, huh." A wicked grin lit his face.

She opened her mouth to reply then closed it, fear snaking down her spine. Her back tingled with it. She was more afraid of her reaction to his sheer maleness than anything else.

"I don't want to hurt you, but I repeat—if you continue to try to escape, I'll be forced to take action."

Her body betrayed her when she thought about him beating her ass the way he beat Appia's. Her clit throbbed again.

He stepped away from her.

She felt relief for the small distance between them. Narrowing her eyes, she scanned his face. A dark, purple bruise lined one side of his jaw. She pointed to his chin. "What happened?" She reached out to touch it, the need to soothe the ugly mark on his strong, angular jaw making her act without thinking.

He grabbed her finger then engulfed her hand in his. She marvelled at how pale hers seemed, locked in his large tanned one. His olive-tone skin gleamed in the light coming in from the window up above.

Her hand shook.

Slowly, Mark drew it towards his mouth. He placed a small, tender kiss on the sensitive skin beneath the underside of her thumb.

She sucked in a breath and swore she could feel the kiss in her breasts and pussy.

"Would that your concern for me be genuine," he murmured. "I would move the skies above to get you away from here and back where you belong." He regarded her thoughtfully. "I want you to know that I have the book in my possession."

She pulled her hand from his. That volume filled with ancient pornography was the ticket to her freedom! It's value, she could only guess, might be thousands of dollars or possibly millions. She could use those funds to pay someone to help her escape.

He eased his tall frame onto the chair across from the bed. He appeared larger than life in that seat. His dark hair was styled in an unusual way, short and close-cropped yet it possessed a wave. The short style accentuated his high cheekbones and angular jaw.

She couldn't stop staring at him, silently cursing for acting like a jackass.

"That book can help you get back home."

Her heart beat wildly.

Maybe Mark had contacts on the outside. If she played her cards right and behaved, he might soften towards her, perhaps, he might feel sorry for her enough so that he would sell the book, and give her the money so she could travel back home.

He drummed his fingers on the arm of the chair. "I don't know if the book, or that stone, will return you to your time, exactly."

"Huh?"

"I must be sure that it won't hurl you into some other era."

"What do you mean, 'some other era'?"

"Surely you realise by now where you are?"

She folded her arms across her breasts. "The Middle East?"

"No."

"Okay, then I'm in Europe."

"Wrong, again." He sighed. "Well, maybe not so wrong, but it is *not* really Europe, *yet.*"

"Well, then, I'm in Turkey?"

He shook his head.

"Then where am I?" Her patience stretched thin. She wanted to strangle him.

"You're in Rome."

"Italy?"

"Yes, but like I said, it really isn't Italy yet."

She sighed. "I have no idea what that means, but I've seen photographs of Rome, they don't look anything like what I've seen out there." She pointed towards the window.

"That's because it is not modern-day Rome."

She raised both brows.

"You time travelled. You are in ancient Rome, in the year AD ninety."

"Riiiiiiiiiight." She nodded. Laughter bubbled up inside her. Soon it leaked out, bit by bit, until she fell back on the bed, rolling with mirth. She held her belly while she giggled.

When she could catch her breath, she gazed at Mark.

He sat still, a muscular tic evident in his jaw. His face bore a dark scowl.

She sat back on her elbows, raising her head to look at him. "You expect me to believe that?"

He scrubbed a hand over his face then rose to his feet. "As crazy as it sounds, yes. You travelled back in time to Ancient Rome."

Her mouth trembled. She bit back a smile and more giggles. Insanity could be a very strange feeling. One minute she cried, the next, she laughed.

The serious look on Mark's face made her wonder just how crazy she'd become. And he looked like he believed his own bullshit. Maybe she wanted to believe it, too. It might be easier than accepting the fact that she now belonged to a white slaver.

"I time travelled to *your* time, to modern-day America," he told her. "I own that bookstore in Cape Cod."

Emotions warred inside her. She didn't know in that moment if she should laugh again...or fucking beat on his chest and cry. If she didn't go along with his lunacy, he'd probably kill her.

Lyla got up from the bed and walked over to the table again. She stroked the rough wood surface. "If I time travelled to ancient Rome, prove it to me." Her pulse quickened. For some odd reason, she really wanted to believe his story.

She hadn't lost her mind yet, for life still felt precious, even if it also seemed tenuous. She'd go along with all this crap for as long as she could stand, and continue to try and escape. As long as breath remained in her body, she would seek to find a way back home.

His face grew thoughtful. "I will prove to you, beyond a shadow of a doubt, that you now reside in Rome, in the year AD ninety."

"And just how are you going to do that?"

He smoothed a hand over her hair then dropped it. His gentle touch almost undid her. Her knees wobbled. He drew his lips into a long, thin line. "After what you see, you will no longer have any doubts."

She rolled her eyes. "I'm loaded with them. And *I* doubt they're going to go away no matter what you try and prove to me."

He folded his arms across his chest, a corner of his sensual mouth lifting into a grin. She liked his arms. They were muscular, with fine hairs lining his forearms.

"Your ornators will prepare you."

"What are 'ornators'?"

"Servants who will bathe and dress you."

"Oh."

It didn't sound so ominous, yet a small zing of fear snaked down her spine when she wondered just who would do the preparing. "I'd uh, prefer to do that myse—"

He placed a finger over her lips. "You do nothing yourself here, Lyla. Not without my consent."

She bristled, but decided she'd better do as he said. "Fine." She folded her arms across her breasts, annoyed that she gave in yet again. "Bring on your ornators." She lifted her chin.

He smiled. "I will thoroughly enjoy my time with you."

"Really?" She raised a brow. "You'll like being with someone who absolutely detests a white slaver like you? Are these ornators of yours preparing me to be sold again?"

He sighed. "No. They will prepare you for your own pleasure." He studied her face for a few seconds. "You've accused me of lying, but now I wonder, just who the impostor really is." He walked out the door and slid it closed behind him.

She lifted a goblet from the basket Appia had brought, intent on throwing it, her patience and nerves stretched to the breaking point. She placed the cup on the table, choosing instead to let it rest there.

Damn, but she hated when he was right.

Away from immediate danger, Lyla would stay safe for the time being inside Mark's home. She glanced at the tunic she wore. Someone had placed it on her yesterday, allowing her to cover her body.

She wondered if Mark did it himself, or if he'd ordered that young girl Appia to dress her.

Lyla looked at the basket. She had food, clothing and security now that she was away from Corvus.

The question that remained was who would keep her safe from her desire for Mark.

Chapter Six

Minutes later, the door opened again, and a small man entered. He spoke in English. "My name is Decimus. I will escort you to the baths."

Her memory stirred. This was the guy who ran to do Mark's bidding after her rescue from Corvus. Lyla determined that if she had to, she could probably knock over this little Decimus shit with one push.

She walked passed him, sailing through the open doorway while she plotted her escape. This Decimus was probably another lackey, doing as the master bade him to do.

"You will feel more refreshed once you've bathed and dressed in more appropriate clothing."

Sure. Uh, huh. Like he cares about my feelings.

She tugged at her dress. While clean, the material scratched her skin, particularly the back of her knees, where the hem ended. She hoped the itching came from the material, and not lice or dirt.

That bath suddenly seemed heavenly, but she had to continue with her escape attempt.

She seized her opportunity, answering in the sweetest voice possible. "How nice. I believe I will feel much better once I've bathed."

"That's the spirit. My master wants what is best for you."

She raised her foot, intent on kicking him in the nuts, but her big toe connected with the little man's shin. Her foot hurt like hell. Despite her poor aim, she at least took him off guard.

Ignoring the pain in her toe, Lyla ran away at breakneck speed.

"Oooooooomph!" The floor came into her line of sight.

Decimus had tackled her from behind.

"Get off me." She struggled beneath him.

Finally, he lifted his weight from her body. Then she rolled on her back.

He stood over her, his arms folded across his chest. Although short, his chest appeared wide. His stance matched it.

He extended his hand. "Come. No more nonsense. Your ornators and bath await."

She got up and turned, but he managed to grab her earlobe.

He pinched it between his fingers. "You are not worth the trouble my master has invested in you."

Her eyes watered as pain shot through her ear. He released his grip and she lifted her hand to massage the fleshy lobe.

"He would punish you thoroughly if he knew what you just did." His scowl turned fierce. "I won't inform him of your childish antics, but let this be a warning to you." He shook his finger at her while he scolded. "If you try anything again, I will tell his Excellency."

He swept his hand out. "Let us proceed to the baths now."

Lyla walked beside him, her steps grudging.

"My master almost lost his life last night, retrieving that book from Corvus."

"He did?"

"It is very dear to him, and from what I can gather, so are you." He stopped walking, turning to face her. "Whether you believe it or not, most of what my master did last evening avenged what Corvus did to you." He lowered his voice. "You'd do well to remember that."

She recalled the bruise on Mark's jaw. He cared enough to avenge her — this side of him was hard to reconcile with his dominating nature... Honour.

They walked on then stopped at the entrance to what appeared to be a large pool.

"Your bath awaits." He gave her a small push on her lower back, propelling her through the entrance.

Her breath caught in her chest when she viewed what Decimus called 'the bath'.

Steam rose from pale blue water while a sweet, intoxicating scent drifted by her nose. Lilies and orchids floated in the pool, making it appear like a tropical paradise. A few chaises resembling day beds were scattered around the bath's perimeter, which was constructed entirely from white marble. Brightly coloured linen cloths lay neatly folded on a table.

Lyla closed her eyes and inhaled the wonderful mix of floral fragrance and something spicy.

When she opened her eyes, they beheld several tall men standing against the walls that circled the bath. Broad-shouldered, with thickly muscled legs and arms, they stood at attention, staring straight ahead.

For just an instant, Lyla wondered if they were real or some strange mannequins. She walked up to one and poked him in the chest. He winked at her.

She jumped back.

When she turned, she noticed two women had entered the bath from an opening on the far side. One had dark sin, her chin-length tresses a mass of tight, precise waves. She wore a long, bright coloured, patterned skirt. A gold necklace draped over her breasts. The long chain hung down to her navel. The other woman had flame-red hair which she wore unbound. It flowed down her shoulders, her naked breasts peeking out from beneath her curls.

The men guarding the bath didn't bat a single eye at the two, half-clad women.

As both females approached, a feeling came over Lyla that she'd seen these two before.

Her eyes widened.

These two women were in the cages across from mine in Corvus' prison!

Her mouth hung open.

The dark girl, the Nubian, stood before her. She tapped Lyla's chin with the tip of her index finger, trailing it down her jaw and throat.

The Nubian's voice held soft notes, even though Lyla couldn't understand what she said. Its deep timber sent shivers of strange, yet, pleasurable tingles down her spine.

The women bowed before her, their shiny tresses gleaming in the muted light overhead from a skylight. They lifted their heads and smiled.

"They are here to serve you, and prepare you for his Excellency," Decimus told Lyla.

She shook her head. "Forget it." She aimed her chin at Decimus. "They don't have to serve me."

Decimus scowled. "But the master requested it. It must be as he commands."

Lyla wanted to rebel, but deep inside her, something gave way. A tiny part of her heart opened, allowing Mark inside.

He kept his promise...

"His Excellency must be obeyed," Decimus stated.

The Nubian reached for Lyla's hand and squeezed it. She touched Lyla's head, in much the same way as Mark did earlier. The redhead reached out and stroked Lyla's shoulder. She lowered her head, but not before a beguiling smile caught Lyla's gaze.

The least I can do is comply with this.

She bit down on her lower lip.

What would it hurt if I did?

She glanced at the pool. It looked inviting. Oh, how she wanted to wash away Corvus and his kidnappers' touches, and the jail's stench.

"I will leave you in Eisha and Corinne's capable hands." Decimus bowed.

She grabbed his arm. "Which one is Eisha and which one is Corinne?"

"Eisha is the Nubian." A corner of his mouth kicked up. "Corinne is the redhead."

Lyla watched him walk out, her heart pounding. She wanted to stop him from leaving, but Eisha and Corinne tugged her dress down her shoulders before she could argue.

They caressed her shoulders.

Lyla shook her head. "No." She backed away from them, the underside of her knees connecting with a low, stone bench.

Corinne reached out and slipped Lyla's tunic down, baring her to the waist.

She sucked in a breath, knowing the men watched. But when she glanced at them, they stood staring straight ahead, their demeanour stoic, their arms crossed over their chests.

"U-nux," the Nubian bent and whispered in Lyla's ear.

"What did you say?" Lyla croaked.

"Unix."

Lyla beetled her brows. Then recognition dawned. "Eunuchs," she stated, her mouth breaking into a grin.

The Nubian nodded her head in agreement.

Lyla sobered. "The poor bastards," she whispered. "I can't believe someone actually castrated them so that they could stand guard here."

Both women helped slide Lyla's tunic down her waist, hips, and legs.

She stood before them butt naked. Warm, humid air surrounded her while the spicy, floral scent filled her nostrils. They grabbed her hands and led her down the steps until she was neck-deep in the warm water.

"Ahhhhhhhhhhhhhhh," slipped from her lips. She loved the feel of the water lapping around her shoulders.

Eisha tipped Lyla's head back. Corinne moved behind her and trickled water over her hair. Then her long fingers massaged her, gently releasing the tension from her head, neck, and shoulders.

Lyla opened her eyes to see Eisha wade through the water. She reached for what looked like a bar of soap and a small sponge sitting on the pool's ledge.

Corinne walked with Lyla over to another end. She helped her up a few steps until they stood in water that came up midway to their thighs. Pushing aside some of Lyla's damp hair, she bathed her neck and chest, trailing the sponge across Lyla's breasts.

Anticipation and lust overcame Lyla. It excited her, but at the same time, shame filled her for enjoying Corinne's touch. She glanced around, hoping to find some means of escape, but the eunuchs would probably catch her and bring her back.

Corinne uttered soothing words in a foreign tongue. Her big, blue eyes matched the water's azure colour.

Eisha approached with a sponge in her hand. She dipped it below the water and drew it between Lyla's thighs.

This time, a sensual tug claimed Lyla's pussy.

The Nubian handed the sponge to the redhead. Corinne slid it across Lyla's upper back, stopping at her bottom.

Lyla's butt tingled from Corinne's touch. She moaned in ecstasy when the sponge slid between the cleft of her ass.

Eisha leaned over and whispered something in Lyla's ear.

"I-I don't understand." Lyla beetled her brows.

Eisha leant down and pushed open Lyla's legs. Then she massaged Lyla's pussy, pressing the sponge gently against her clit.

Lyla reached out and gripped Eisha's shoulders.

Corinne slipped her arms around Lyla's waist. Her lips grazed her neck.

Lyla shuddered, but not from the cool air touching her skin, it was the feel of Corinne's lips on her throat.

The more Eisha rubbed, the more that deep, sensual ache filled Lyla's body. A fluttering sensation filled her belly, signalling the start of an orgasm.

Corinne massaged Lyla's ass cheeks, passing the tip of her index finger up and down the opening there. She didn't invade her bottom, but reached between Lyla's legs to touch her pussy that showed there.

Her legs shook with each touch.

Eisha reached up and kissed Lyla's breasts, suckling her nipples between her lips.

"Ohhhhhhhhhhhhhh!" Lyla cried, her orgasm so intense, it left her breathless. Her spent body almost folded.

Eisha and Corinne helped her back into the deeper water, uttering soothing, calming words Lyla didn't understand, but the tone of their voices took away all her fears.

They washed her hair next, allowing her to come back down to earth as they massaged a fragrant soap through her tresses. After rinsing her thoroughly, they helped her from the pool, drying her with two large pieces of linen. Then they laid her down on a padded bench, turning her over until she lay on her belly.

Something warm trickled down her back. A new fragrance, like orchids, drifted by her nose.

The two women massaged the oil into the skin of her back and legs, making her feel like a limp noodle when they finished. They turned her over and massaged her. Their deft hands slid across her breasts, between her legs, over her thighs and knees, working their way down her shins. They lifted each foot, kissing her big toes, and kneaded them as well.

Lyla moaned in ecstasy when they massaged her instep and the crook of her big toe.

When they were finished, they brought her to a small dressing room, where they outfitted her in a white silk gown with a deep neckline. It exposed her chest and breasts, revealing her nipples. They lifted and piled her hair into an up-do, then adorned it with tiny, purple flowers. Red vegetable dye adorned Lyla's lips and cheeks, just enough to bring some colour into her face.

She slipped her feet into a pair of sandals with delicate straps that crossed the top of her foot.

Corinne held a polished, metal mirror before Lyla.

She gasped at her reflection. Eisha and Corinne had transformed her into a beautiful, breathtaking, Roman woman.

No one would guess she hailed from modern-day America.

She shook her head at her insane thoughts.

She still lived in modern-day times.

Or...did she?

It had to be mind conditioning forcing her to forget her real self.

Or maybe, she finally saw who she really was...

The woman she always wanted to be.

Chapter Seven

A little while later, two eunuchs escorted Lyla into an atrium.

Mark's eyes met hers when she entered the small yard brimming with flowers and fountains. He murmured something in his odd foreign language. The men left, and for just a second, Lyla thought she finally recognised the tone and cadence of the words Mark spoke.

It sounded like Latin.

His look grew hot when he perused her gown's plunging neckline. He nodded his head. "It suits you. Eisha and Corinne did well." He walked around her, stopping to stand directly before her. His eyes settled on her chest.

Before she knew what he intended, he leant down and kissed it.

She held her breath while his mouth caressed her right nipple. Lyla ran her fingers through his thick, dark, hair, gripping his head between her hands. She loved the hot brand of his mouth.

Hated it, too.

It was the same feeling of lust and shame she experienced with Eisha and Corinne. Her face flamed when she thought about what she did with them. She took a deep breath then stepped away from Mark. "So, what are your plans to prove to me that I am in ancient Rome?"

"I will take you someplace that will suck the breath from your body."

Lyla raised a brow. "Your bedroom?"

He tipped back his head and laughed. "Lyla, you are a joy." His eyes darkened. "Come here," he commanded.

Her pussy vibrated from his voice's rough timber.

She walked over to where he stood. Before she could utter any objection, he clamped a wide, metal collar around her neck.

She pulled and tugged at the band.

He placed his hand over hers. "Leave it. It will not come off until I command that it does."

"What is this, this—" While it didn't choke her, she panicked when she couldn't remove it.

He brought her over to the fountain. "Look at your reflection in the water."

The collar was studded with beautiful coloured gemstones, including clear stones that looked like diamonds. They gleamed in the light, their startling beauty reflected in the water. The collar didn't appear as wide as she initially thought, but it still accentuated her long neck, the gems a wonderful accent to her pale skin, now flushed with a pink tinge.

"You must wear it when we go out, so that no one will take you from me."

"You're insane if you think I'm going to wear this." She tugged at the collar, but it wouldn't budge.

"Stop. You'll hurt that lovely skin on your throat." Mark covered her hand with his. "I know that now you do not wear it willingly —"

"I'll *never* wear it by choice!" Tears clogged her throat.

"You will. One day. I know you will."

"You're overplaying your hand. Don't think you know me so well, because you don't."

He gave her a dark look. "Be that as it may, we are going on a little trip."

"Where?" Panic suddenly filled her. *Is he going to sell me again?*

"You'll just have to wait and see."

* * * *

A few minutes later, she stood outside on the walkway, in front of Mark's home. The crowded street resembled New York City on a hot summer day, with vendors, stalls and tons of visitors strolling along.

Several men brought Mark's litter to where she stood. They rested it on the ground.

"Get in, Lyla," Mark ordered.

"No." Memories of what happened in it the last time surfaced. She'd truly be a wanton slut if she succumbed to her feelings for him. Besides, the men carrying it looked as if they were about to pass out from the intense heat.

Mark scanned the crowded sidewalk. "Do as I say. This is not the time to argue with me."

"Why don't you let me know when the time is right? I'll be ready."

His voice dipped. "For debating...or making love with me?"

She raised her chin, but it shook. Damn, but he made her mad with lust. *Yup. I am crazy!*

"Give them some water."

He furrowed his brow. "Who?"

She nodded towards the slaves. "The men who will be toting us around. At least give them something cool to drink. They look like they're ready to drop dead." When she glanced at Mark's face, he didn't look pleased.

His scowl turned deep and forbidding. Then he turned to his steward. "Do as she asks."

The little man, Decimus, just stood there, staring at Mark like he had lost his mind completely.

"Now," Mark commanded. "Give them water now."

The little man bowed. "As you wish, Excellency."

People walked by, giving Mark and Lyla curious looks.

Mark flexed his right hand by his side. "You've chosen to make a wonderful spectacle of yourself."

She gave him a cheeky grin. "Why, thank you." It gave her satisfaction to know that she bested him. *This time.*

"This isn't a game. You're my slave, my *lupa*. You're beautiful and desirable, and I don't need any man getting ideas about you."

That took the wind from her sales. He thought her beautiful? Desirable?

He grabbed her upper arm. Leaning down, he whispered in her ear, "If you don't get in the damned litter, I'm going to make a *spectacle* of beating your bare ass right here, out in the street."

Her pussy throbbed so hard her knees almost buckled. She remained upright and steady on her feet, lest he see how weak his heated threat made her feel. She wasn't afraid, damn it, she was turned on. But she wouldn't let him see that, either.

She schooled her features and got into the litter, scooting all the way over to the far right corner.

He got in afterwards.

Decimus leaned in and asked, "Will that be all, Excellency?" He held a pitcher in his hand. Several water droplets leaked out.

Lyla gave him a two-finger salute, grinning all the while.

He cast a dark look at her.

"We are off on our journey, Decimus," Mark stated.

Lyla snorted.

Mark rolled his eyes.

"Good luck to you, Master." Decimus shook his head. Lowering his voice, he finished by saying, "You're going to need it."

"I heard that." Lyla jabbed a finger in his direction.

"May the gods be with you, Excellency."

The litter started to move. Lyla held onto the sides until it settled into a comfortable gait. No linen blocked her view this time. She saw the teeming, crowded streets of the city while they made their way towards their destination.

"I wanted you to see this clearly. There is no way I could possibly fabricate something like this."

"No, you just drugged me, so I *believe* I'm seeing ancient Rome," Lyla huffed.

Maybe this is some elaborate movie set... But deep down, she wasn't so sure.

He shook his head. "I do not drug women."

"No, you kidnap them first, then you drug them."

"I've done nothing like that to you."

Lyla marvelled at the magnificent residences, one more splendid than the other. The din from the crowd grew louder. She almost wished the damned linen were back on the opening. It might have drowned out the noise from the street.

Lyla held her nose in one particular section they passed through. "It smells like rotten eggs."

"Not exactly the nicest part of town," Mark answered. "There's a slaughterhouse here."

She pitied the animals.

She looked out the window, noticing garbage lining the street. "It's filthy."

"Not all people in Rome reside in wealth, but don't worry, we'll be at the coliseum soon."

She sat back against the padded headrest. "Riiiiiiiight."

"When you see it, you will understand that this is no crazy dream, and no illusion. When you time travel, you sometimes think that what you're seeing and doing is from your wildest imaginings."

"So, you're a tried and true time traveller?"

"As was my father."

"Like father, like son," she replied in a singsong voice.

He shook his head. "I am beginning to see how sarcastic you really are. It is meant to push people away."

"How very astute, Doctor Freud."

He narrowed his eyes. "I know no such person. Do I remind you of this 'doctor'?" A muscle ticked in his jaw. Something sparked in his eyes, then they deepened until they turned black.

She could have sworn he became jealous at the mention of another man she knew. Lyla enjoyed tweaking that one dangerous emotion. "If you did know about Doctor Freud, you'd remember him as the father of what's called 'modern psychology'."

He whipped his head around. "He's your *father*?"

She bit back a smile. "No. Of modern psychology."

"Psyche," he mused. "That is an old Greek word that means the human mind or soul."

"Ah, so you must have read those books you sold in that sham of a store. Is that what you did? Used it as a 'front' so you could kidnap women like me and sell them on the open market?"

"It is not a sham. I thirst for knowledge. And I've told you many times, I do not deal in slavery that way."

"Appia said you bought her from Corvus."

"I did. Anything to get her away from *him*."

She slumped back in her seat, thinking about Appia's fate. "You're going to sell her, in turn, to some wealthy man?"

"Who told you that?"

She bit down on her lower lip, wanting to keep her conversation with Appia a secret. If Mark knew she had spoken to Appia about all this, he'd probably punish the girl. "I, uh, just thought you were."

He scowled. "I'm grooming Appia so that she can marry my friend who travels extensively on business."

"And why is that?"

"I would hope that she could see her family again. My friend, Cletus, does much trade with Greece."

Her mouth hung open. "D-does she know that?"

"I did not want to raise her hopes, in case this marriage does not come to pass, but Cletus is fascinated with her. He will treat her well. Even though Appia is a slave, it doesn't matter to him. He will go along with the story I invented that she is my cousin through marriage, living with me since her parents died."

Suddenly, she sat forward. "Oh. My." She stuck her head out of the litter. "God," she finished.

Lyla sucked in a breath while she viewed the scene before her. The ancient Roman coliseum rose thousands of feet into the air, directly before her.

The litter slowed. Then the men placed it on the ground.

She didn't wait for Mark, but scrambled from her seat before he could say a word. One of the men who carried the litter ran over to assist her.

Her eyes fixed on the breathtaking spectacle.

"Amphitheatrum Flavium," the slave told her.

She whispered in reply, her hand moving to her throat, "It's unbelievable."

The structure spanned acres. She couldn't stop her gaze from travelling upwards. It seemed as though thousands of intricately carved columns and spaces resembling windows lined the huge elliptical structure. She could see thousands of people walking, even on the highest tiers.

The slave bowed before her. He didn't look so haggard. Maybe the water revived him. "Gratias ago vos," he told her.

She sighed, not understanding what he said. She glanced back at Mark.

"He says, 'thank you', Lyla."

"Anytime you need water, just ask me," she told the slave.

The slave gave her a questioning look, but bowed just the same.

Do they ever get tired of bowing and scraping before everyone?

Mark exited the litter and joined her. "You are to stay by my side while we're here." He grabbed her upper arm and toted her along.

"Why not just attach a leash to this thing?" She pointed to her collar.

He gave her a wicked smile. "It does have a little hook on it just for that reason."

He always took the wind from her sails.

"If you try to escape, I *will* be forced to add a tether. The coliseum gets crowded. People come from miles around to see the entertainment here. On a good day, it can hold up to fifty-five thousand people."

The streets teemed with spectators crowding into the seventy-six numbered entrances.

"This is just like the Nassau Coliseum and Madison Square Garden."

"The what?"

"The sports arenas I've been to for concerts and games."

"Trust me." He hustled her along. "This place is *nothing* like those arenas. There's a lot of riff-raff here and very unsavoury characters."

She stepped over a man lying on his back on the sidewalk.

"The drinking starts early."

She nodded. "Too much tailgating."

"Too much what?" He cocked his head.

"Never mind." She sighed.

He whisked her into an entrance that wasn't numbered.

"How come we're going in here?" she asked.

"It's reserved for dignitaries."

She walked beside him as they found their seats away from the poorer classes.

Around her sat a crowd. The women dressed in exquisite gowns of different colours, one more daring than the next. One woman's garment was cut in a bias off the shoulder, revealing a single, perfect breast. The man sitting next to her took a draught of something in a metal goblet then leant down to kiss the woman's nipple. She squealed with delight.

"I thought you said this section is reserved for dignitaries?" She plopped down on a hard marble seat next to Mark.

"It is."

The women's faces were heavily painted with make-up. Some had servants fanning them with large feathers and some had slaves who held fancy umbrellas over their heads, shielding them from the sun.

Soon, the entire ancient arena filled with spectators.

She looked upwards to see a purple linen awning being drawn over the crowd. "How are they doing that?"

"It is the 'velarium' used to protect us from the sun's heat and inclement weather. It is a canopy positioned over posts that are located at the top of the amphitheatre."

"I-I have never seen anything like it," she murmured. The stench of perspiring bodies assailed her nose. She hoped a breeze would drift by and take the odour with it.

She rose from her seat. "Let's go sit somewhere else. It stinks here." She screwed up her face.

Mark pulled her down. Her bottom hit the marble, making her realise just how uncomfortable the seats really were. No wonder everyone sat around drinking wine. It dulled the sensation of being sore, hot, and smelly.

She wanted to be home in New York.

Badly.

She missed the automobile traffic sounds, rock and roll music, and modern people. She hated the men and women surrounding her now. They were noisy and garish and possessed little concern for those around them, giving in to their most base desires.

Maybe she hated it so much because nothing much had changed in a couple of thousand years. Many people back home reminded her of these idiots.

A sudden urge came upon her. Damn, but she had to use the bathroom.

He frowned. "Are you all right?"

"I-I have to pee."

He gave her a hard stare. "Lyla, if this is another ploy to try and escape me, I'll—"

"It's not." She wiggled on the seat. "I really have to, um, go. To the bathroom, that is." Her face heated.

He held up two fingers at a boy who looked to be no older than twelve. He walked over to Lyla, bearing something that resembled a porcelain pot.

Mark flipped a coin at the young man. He caught it deftly and handed her the vessel.

She frowned. "What am I supposed to do with that?"

"You said you had to relieve yourself."

"Yes, but—" Her eyes widened. "Do you mean I've got to use that thing?"

"Of course."

"No, I'm going to the ladies room." She got up again.

He pulled her back down. "The toilets are filthy here. Use the damned pot and stop attracting attention."

"Oh, like using this thing…" She held it up to examine it. A foul odour assailed her nostrils. She turned her head away and grimaced. "Won't attract attention."

He ripped the pot from her hand. "Put it under your gown and do what you have to." He looked like he wanted to kill her.

Her extreme urge to relieve herself overtook any fear. She sat up a little, hiked up her gown, and then positioned the pot between her legs. When she was finished, she handed it back to the boy.

He walked away, intent on finding his next customer.

God help me, how in hell do they let children do these horrible jobs? "His mother shouldn't let him do something like that. He should be in school," she grumbled.

"School," Mark repeated, his face thoughtful.

"Yes, school. Why isn't he there?"

"Because he has to work. Whatever money he earns probably goes to his family."

"That's terrible!"

"It serves a purpose. You acquire, uh, comfort, let's say." Her face reddened.

"And he gets the coin he needs to survive."

"That's archaic and awful and—"

"Someone has to do it."

"Not a child!"

"Lyla, you'd do well to remember that in your world, slavery still exists. It's still around in your time, but people don't like to talk about it. Just like they don't want to talk about it now." The discussion closed, but not in Lyla's mind.

She couldn't let go of Mark's statement about child slavery. Children were still sold into slavery in her world. They became indentured servants, something she thought long gone since backward, feudal times.

She suddenly remembered reading an article about a young girl, a 'household slave' to some family in California. *Some things never change...*

Bitterness overcame her. If she escaped this horrid land, she vowed to break the shackles of slavery that trapped many of the world's children.

Mark rose to his feet. "Come." He extended his hand. "There is someone you must meet."

She took his hand, her curiosity piqued. "Who?"

"My cousin." He led her over to a grand spectator's box where several people sat.

In the middle of them all, a man graced a throne. The fancy chair appeared to be solid gold. The man sitting in it seemed as tall as Mark, his nose almost identical, the bump the same.

His haughty demeanour reflected his arrogance and conceit. Atop his head, he wore a crown of gold leaves. His deep purple toga covered what she thought to be a muscular, well-toned body.

She shivered in response to the look that passed between them. As though he wanted to *eat* her.

"*Dominus et Deus.*" Mark dropped to one knee and bowed low.

Lyla whispered from the corner of her mouth, "What did you say to him?"

"I addressed him as Master and God."

"Just who does this guy think he is?" She folded her arms across her chest.

"Emperor Domitian."

She blinked once, then her eyes widened. "Do you mean to tell me, the *emperor* is your cousin?"

"Unfortunately, yes." Mark grimaced, answering her from the side of *his* mouth.

Domitian squinted at Lyla, then motioned with his hand for her to come forwards.

Mark rose and gave her a push in her lower back. "Do as he says."

"Why does he keep squinting? The sun's not shining in his eyes."

"He has trouble seeing."

"So, he should get glasses or conta—" She sighed. "I know. I *know*. Eyeglasses haven't been invented yet." She walked towards Domitian's grand throne. He raised a brow.

She curtsied quickly then rose to her feet. She couldn't help but cast him a sour look.

He rested his forearms on the chair and scowled, speaking rapidly to Mark in Latin.

She looked back at Mark.

"Go on," he told her.

"Go on...*what*?"

"He wants to touch your hair."

"Oh, for Pete's sake..."

"Just, do it, Lyla!"

She took two steps forward.

Domitian put his hand on her head, stroking his fingers through her hair. Then he smiled. He addressed Mark again. They spoke quickly. Domitian's brows shot up when Mark mentioned Corvus. They spoke again, the one word she heard repeated was 'lupa'.

Domitian shook his head, uttering something.

Mark bowed slightly.

"What did he say?" She elbowed Mark in the ribs.

He pushed her hand to her side. "He commanded that Corvus should be watched. Whatever belonged to my *lupa,*" he drew out the word. "Belongs to me. Domitian is not happy with Corvus right now."

"Corvus seems to be a very unpopular guy around here."

"He is a *lenones,* the most vile slave trader. He sells women into prostitution. A portion of his profits goes directly to the empire."

"You mean, Domitian?"

"Precisely. But Domitian would not want that to get around."

Domitian motioned with his hand towards Lyla. He spoke rapidly again.

"Well, what does he want now?"

"He says, What is your name, pet?"

Ohhhhhhhhhhhhhhh, what she wouldn't like to do to *Domitian!* Her hand flexed at her side. She wadded it into a fist, but Mark threaded his fingers through hers, pushing her hand open.

"Stay calm," he whispered to her. "He's just baiting you."

"Lyla." Her voice rang out. "My name is Lyla." She lifted her chin.

A collective gasp went up from the small crowd fawning over Domitian.

"Say, *dominus et deus.*" Mark whispered to her.

"He thinks rather highly of himself, doesn't he?"

"Just say it, damn you."

She bowed before Domitian and said in a tight voice, "Dominus et Deus."

Domitian grinned, then dismissed them.

Back at their seats, Lyla fumed. "Of all the arrogant, pig-headed, ohhhhhhhhhhh, I can't think of enough nasty things to say about him." She shook her head, grinding a fist into her thigh.

"Be quiet and wave. He's looking at us."

She pasted a bright smile on her face and wiggled her fingers in Domitian's direction.

"He's right, you know. I should take you in hand." Mark grinned.

"He said *that?*"

"Uh, huh." Mark's smile turned wicked.

It did strange things to her belly. She buffeted him in the arm. "Like I would let you."

He leaned over and kissed her chest, his tongue flicking her nipple.

"Oh, my…" she moaned in ecstasy, her face heating. "We-we're in a p-public place." She could barely speak.

"Domitian needs to understand that you're mine," Mark growled. He kissed her breasts.

"Why?" She had trouble concentrating.

Mark's mouth worked its way across one breast, to the other. "He might try and take you from me."

She stilled.

"People know that if you receive an invitation to dine with the emperor, and you bring your wife, daughters, or any other woman from your household, Domitian will make love to them that night."

"*Are you serious?*"

"Very. Domitian may do as he chooses."

"The beast."

Mark tugged on her dress, fingering her other nipple.

She almost came right there on the seat.

"And you, my sweet, bring out the beast in me."

A trumpet sounded. Two gladiators entered the arena.

Lyla clamped a hand over her mouth when the first blow landed, sending a stream of blood spurting through the air.

Mark rarely visited the coliseum, except to pay the occasional tribute to his cousin, who seemed to love everything about it.

A collective shout went out when one gladiator lopped off his opponent's arm.

Lyla buried her head in his shoulder. "I can't watch this."

He made a silent vow to protect her from everyone and everything that would harm her. She had yet to understand and accept the danger of his ancient time.

Reluctantly, he lifted her face from his shoulder and made her watch the two men in the arena. He wanted to turn away from it all, but if he did, Lyla would sense his weakness. He needed her to know that he would protect her from men like Corvus and Domitian, but she had to see, and believe, everything that happened from this point on.

"This is no different than watching the violence on modern American television," he stated with far more certainty than he felt.

Lyla's pale face and wide, unblinking eyes tore at his heart. "How can you say that?" She shook her head, her lips trembling.

He longed to kiss her to stop their shaking, but it would make things worse—for him, as well as her.

"These are two men trying to k-kill each other. It's horrible."

"You want me to think that it doesn't go on in your time?" He raised a brow.

She looked around at the audience. "Everyone here seems so immune to what's happening. It is nothing but entertainment for them."

"Just like watching all the terrible things on television and in the movies in *your* time. People are just as impervious to violence in the modern world."

"Yes, but movies and television aren't real. What we're seeing here *is*."

He raised a brow. "But do you turn away from the violence you view on television, whether real or fake? No, you don't. In fact, what you're seeing many times is actual, violent footage in real time. Admit it, when you see that, aren't you just a bit fascinated? As gory as it may seem, as ugly or brutal as it may be, you don't turn away. A perverse interest overtakes you."

She couldn't argue with him. For once, she didn't come back with a snappy retort. Maybe because she realised what he said was the truth. The modern world was just as fascinated by violence.

When the show ended, a decapitated man lay on the amphitheatre floor in a bloody heap. The crowd roared. They rose to their feet cheering and shouting, while the triumphant gladiator held his sword high in the air, proclaiming victory.

The tip of the sword held the dead man's head.

Mark caught Lyla before she hit the ground, her eyes rolling backwards, her body limp in his arms.

Chapter Eight

Later, outside the coliseum, Lyla sucked in huge gulps of air. Bile rose in her throat. It tasted bitter and burned when she attempted to swallow it. Nausea rose in her belly.

A slave who carried the litter brought her a small metal cup filled with water. He glanced towards the other three slaves who stood by the litter, awaiting orders. They bowed their heads in her direction.

She gulped the water down, and handed the cup back to the slave. "Th-thank you," she murmured.

The man nodded, then walked over to join his companions.

Mark took her arm and helped her inside the litter.

Her body and mind were weak. Drained. Devoid of emotion.

If she squeezed her eyes closed, she could erase that ugly scene of the headless corpse. *That poor man!*

The problem was it kept coming back, no matter how hard she tried to forget it. The drive home grew tedious and long. She didn't speak. When she tried to form an entire sentence, her mind drifted. She couldn't concentrate.

A terrible thought finally permeated her brain, an idea more horrible than the bloody gore she witnessed earlier. This was not a hoax. She had been hurled backwards in time to ancient Rome. Maybe, Mark did possess some strange power that enabled him time travel.

Moreover, perhaps his story held truth about her stroking some weird stone on the cover of that book. Perhaps the book possessed a force that propelled her back in time when she touched it.

By the time the litter arrived at Mark's home, cold seeped into her pores. She trembled, her shudders increasing until her entire body shook uncontrollably.

Mark removed his toga, placing it over her shoulders. It trailed down to the floor, engulfing her small frame with warmth and his exotic, unique smell. He held out his hand.

She placed hers in it and looked down on their joined hands. Tears filled her eyes. She didn't know why she cried, but she couldn't seem to stop.

He led her to a room with a low table set in the centre. A fountain stood nearby, the sound of the running water soothing her taut nerves. He eased her down onto some cushions then clapped his hands.

Soon, Appia appeared, as well as two young men.

Mark gave them orders in Latin.

Afterwards, they ran from the room to do his bidding.

She pulled Mark's cape tightly around her body, hoping it would warm her.

"Lyla," he murmured. "Sit with me."

She shook her head. Tears clogged her throat, making it difficult for her to speak.

He patted his thighs.

She looked over at his lap. It looked wide and inviting. She scrambled over to him, the cape tangling around her legs.

He caught her to him and gently placed her on his thighs.

Soon, the food came. The odour of warm bread and grilled meat drifted by her nose. She didn't think she could eat a single bite.

Mark held a goblet by her nostrils. A fruity aroma revived her. She sipped from the cup and realised it was not the sour, watered down wine she'd had when she first arrived.

This drink tasted delicious. She swirled the deep red liquid in her mouth, enjoying the combined flavours of grape, berries, and oak.

He raised the cup to her lips again. She drank some more. Then he fed her some sliced fruit. It resembled and tasted like a juicy, ripe pear. In between, he gave her small bites of a spicy pepper, marinated in something salty.

The creamy texture and savoury taste of soft cheese took away the pepper's sting, but the heat from the spicy vegetable invaded her body, warming her and enabling her to focus.

She looked up at Mark's handsome face, taut with worry.

"I'm sorry you had to see that in the arena." He told her. "But you needed to believe the reality surrounding you."

Her body was aflame because of the wine and spicy peppers. Or maybe, it was Mark.

Lyla slipped the toga from her shoulders. To eradicate the horrible vision of that dead, headless man from her mind, she needed to replace it with something else.

The desire to live, to mate, hit her full force. She needed to reaffirm life after that nightmare she'd witnessed.

She reached for another piece of fruit, but he was quicker, popping the slice into her mouth. She savoured the juice running down her throat.

Then he fed her some grilled meat. It tasted delectable, like roast pork.

"Lyla, I will give you anything, do anything, to ease the burden of what you saw today. Whatever you desire, your pleasure will be fulfilled."

She fingered the collar around her neck, noticing her reflection when she glanced into the side of a polished, metal wine goblet. The jewels encrusted in the wide, metal strip glittered in the light.

Her boldness returned, bit by precious bit. Instead of the collar making her feel subservient like it did earlier, it suddenly made her feel beautiful.

What is my pleasure, he had asked.

She wanted him to dominate her completely. She needed release and she wanted it now. She threw aside fear, and decided to jump headfirst into what she desired.

"Trust me to make you happy, Lyla. I will give you the greatest pleasure you've ever experienced. If there's something I do that you don't like, you'll tell me and I will stop. I promise."

She sighed. "Promises are easily broken."

"Not mine."

The first wall around Lyla's heart crumbled. She perused his face and body, while he stretched lazily on the cushions. He reminded her of a big, wild cat.

As the barricades surrounding her heart started to fall, her body overflowed with lust. She wondered if he laced the wine with a drug, for her clit throbbed with such intensity, she thought she'd go mad.

Oh, how I want to jump his bones!

"You'll give me a signal. One word, and I'll stop immediately. I promise, Lyla."

"Horny."

He frowned. "You're hor—?" His mouth lifted into a smile. "Oh, I see. That's the word you want to use. 'Horny'."

"Uh, huh." Her heart raced. She jumped when he clapped his hands together, the sound echoing through the room.

Soon, four big men stood before them.

Lyla recognised them instantly. They were the four slaves that had carried the litter. The one who gave her the water at the Coliseum bowed his head then his eyes caught hers.

She had the most insane desire to preen naked before them...and Mark. Her breasts were suddenly too heavy for her body. Her nipples ached for the touch of the slave's lips. Shame washed over her. *How can I be thinking such wicked thoughts about that man?*

"I am going to watch while they pleasure you, Lyla," Mark told her.

Her nipples peaked. They pushed against her gown.

Mark's eyes were drawn to her chest.

She looked at the four, swarthy, well-built servants, wishing their mouths were on her breasts right now.

"Whatever you wish them to do, they will." Mark nodded at the four men.

"They're going to serve me? How?"

He glanced at the four men. "Their task is to pleasure you."

She gave a mental shake and bit down on her lower lip. She could never seem to handle one man back home, let alone four. If she counted Mark in the mix, that made five. The idea of allowing those four slaves to pleasure her before Mark sent her heart and pulse racing like a runaway train.

Mark helped her to her feet then moved to stand behind her. His warm breath scattered the few tendrils of hair that escaped her up-do. They drifted against her skin, tickling it. That feeling drove shivers down her back.

"I will not let them harm you, Lyla," Mark whispered in her ear. He nipped her lobe with his teeth.

"Ohhhhhhhhhhhh." She tipped her head back to rest against his shoulder, closing her eyes.

He fondled her breasts, massaging the tender tips. When she opened her eyes, she saw that Mark signalled to one man.

He approached.

Mark commanded the slave to do something.

Lyla wished she understood! But her lack of knowledge fuelled fear and excitement about the unknown.

The slave tugged on her gown, exposing both breasts. Then he bent his head. She sucked in a breath when his tongue touched her right nipple. Then he blew on it, the breeze surrounding her turgid little point sending arrows of need straight down to her labia.

Her knees buckled, but Mark caught her before she slipped to the floor. He released her then he positioned himself on the cushions. His eyes remained on Lyla, his gaze hot.

Standing there before him made her taut with worry, but at the same time, it heightened her anticipation.

The other three slaves approached. Lyla's palms grew damp. Perspiration inched down her back.

Slowly, one of the slaves removed her gown, sliding it down her shoulders. They tugged it over her hips, allowing it to pool at her feet. She had stood naked in Corvus' prison and was deeply humiliated.

Yet, here, standing before Mark and these men, she could be...free. Like she could soar high into the air on sensual wings of pleasure.

Another slave knelt before her. He parted her thighs then licked her cunt.

"Ahhhhhhhhhhhh!" Lyla gripped his shoulders.

He passed his tongue across her clit again. She spread her legs wider, pressing her pussy against his mouth.

He kissed and suckled her little pleasure bud, drawing it into his mouth for several seconds then released it.

"I-I have to come," she moaned. Release seemed seconds away, she could let go now, or...

"Not yet, my sweet," Mark told her.

She looked over at him, his long legs stretched out before him. He popped a grape into his mouth chewed then swallowed. She watched his prominent Adam's apple bob up and down. She also noticed the bulge in his groin. His penis pushed against his tunic.

The balance of control lay within her. Never, in all her other sexual relationships with any man, did she ever feel this potent. It made her head spin.

"Hold back your release until I command you to come," Mark stated.

She did as he told her, biting down on her lower lip to distract her body, and her mind, from coming. In that instant, she hated Mark for making her restrain herself.

"I know you don't like it." He chuckled. "I can tell from that stormy look on your face."

"You're enjoying this, aren't you?"

"Immensely." His grin became wicked.

She panted, hoping that the quick intake and exhalation would hold her release at bay. She wanted to show him that she could persevere.

"Good girl," he crooned. "You are doing well."

Pride filled her, Mark's praise heightening the feel of the slave's mouth against her pussy. She squirmed against his lips. "Can I come now?" she asked Mark.

"No."

"Why not?" She panted again.

"'Master' is how you must address me."

"Master, why can't I come?"

"Because I haven't given you permission to do so."

She took more short, shallow breaths. Mark spoke to the slaves and pointed to a padded bench. The slave lifted his mouth from her cunt.

"No!" she cried. She wanted more of his lips and tongue.

"You will enjoy this, Lyla, I promise," Mark told her.

The two slaves escorted her over to the piece of furniture. Her thighs quivered. They bent her over it so that her ass was on display for Mark.

The fact that she couldn't see him intensified her anticipation. Eagerness and curiosity overruled any hesitation. She wanted to know what they would do to her next, remembering her 'safe' word...and Mark's promise not to hurt her.

Catherine Chernow

Mark clapped his hands again. She watched as one of the slaves walked towards a small table and retrieved an ewer. The slave stepped behind her.

Mark bent over her and whispered near her ear. "When we were in Corvus' viewing room, I sensed that you were a virgin, here, in your *solum*." He patted her ass, running his finger along the cleft between her butt cheeks.

Her clit throbbed in response. "Yessssssssss," she moaned. "I am."

"No man has ever had this pleasure, and that gives me great satisfaction."

She sucked in a breath when his warm, slippery hands massaged her ass. Her desire increased when she noticed the slaves watching her. Two men held her firmly in place, her belly against the padded seat. The other two stared directly into her eyes.

Mark continued to massage her bottom, running his hands across her skin. "It will not be like Corvus' jail. I intend to get you accustomed to the feel of my fingers in your *solum*."

He continued to stroke her bottom. Then he eased his index finger inside her. He held it there for a few seconds, allowing her to get used to it. He didn't shove it in any farther. He didn't move it.

She sucked in a breath then released it.

"Does it give you pleasure, Lyla?"

"Yes," she murmured.

"Be truthful," he whispered in her ear.

"It seems as though you're filling me entirely. I like it. "

He removed it slowly, but the absence of his finger in her bottom made her feel empty, deep inside.

"That's enough for now," he commanded.

The two slaves helped her rise from the bench.

Mark took her face between his hands and kissed her. His breath tasted sweet and a little like wine. "I will not take your bottom now. It is not something one leaps into."

"I wasn't afraid," she replied, her voice resonating through the chamber. She didn't have any fear in her body in that minute, just desire.

"I'm glad you trust me," he told her.

Did she really trust him, she wondered. Or was he the one port in a stormy sea? No, she wouldn't let doubt creep in.

He turned her in his arms so that he could massage her breasts before the slaves. Their hot, watchful gaze filled her with lust.

Her hands possessed a mind of their own. She reached down, and stroked her cunt. She watched their cocks rise beneath their tunics.

Mark stopped her. "Never touch yourself there unless I command you to."

Irritation sounded in her voice. "But I want to come. In full view of everyone."

"When I say so."

She could argue. She wanted to. She wanted to push Mark to his limit, but held off. There'd be plenty of time to best him. Right now, she wanted more release.

She bowed her head. "As you wish, Master." Then she lifted her face to his and looked him right in the eyes, hoping he noticed the challenge *hers* held.

Mark uttered a command to a slave, then pointed to her groin. The slave walked over to her then dropped to his knees and suckled her cunt. Those lovely sensations inched downwards, settling in her toes. She wiggled them in response.

"Lean over him, hold on to his shoulders."

Lyla did as Mark ordered, her hands digging into the bony ridges between the man's wide shoulders and neck. Her pussy grew damp and slick from the action of the slave's mouth and tongue against her pleasure zone.

She heard something, a strange sound from behind her. It was a crinkling noise, followed by snapping. She looked back to see Mark slip a condom on his penis.

"It is the muscle tissue of a man slaughtered in battle."

Her eyes widened.

"He gave his life bravely for the empire. This piece of him will protect you, have no fear."

She held her breath while he slipped his sheathed cock inside her labia from behind. She revelled in the sensation as his big, thick cock made its way in. The damned condom was ribbed!

He moved, just a bit, sliding in, then out. With the slave going down on her cunt, and Mark taking her from behind, she didn't know if she could hold her orgasm back.

"Come when I command you, Lyla."

"Ohhhhhhhhhhh. I have to come. Now." She bit down on her lower lip.

He rode her some more. The slave lapped at her pussy.

"Please, Mark."

"Address me properly."

"Master," she hissed, throwing her head back against his shoulder.

He massaged her breasts, tweaking her nipples gently with the pads of his fingers. "Now, you may come."

Her orgasm exploded within her. She tried to draw it out for as long as she could, the wonderful sensations overtaking her body. She folded, clutching the slave's

head, while a wave of exquisite delight flowed over her.
When it passed, she turned her head and glanced at Mark.
He smiled.

And so, she discovered, did she.

Chapter Nine

Marcus dismissed the four slaves. As much as he enjoyed sharing Lyla and delighting in her pleasure at their hands, he wanted her all to himself now.

She lay sprawled against the cushions, her nude body relaxed and replete. The tiny purple flowers remained in her tresses, but her mass of flaxen hair had come loose and tumbled around her shoulders in waves. The ends trailed down her shoulders and breasts. Her creamy skin and exquisite, rounded form made her appear like a goddess.

He never believed the Roman mythology, but Lyla could make him change his mind.

He slid next to her and whispered, "Vos es meus decor , meus dulcis."

"What does it mean?"

"You are my beauty, my sweet."

She smiled at him, her mouth wide her eyes dreamy.

He leant down and captured her lips with his own, branding her further in a heated kiss that made his loins pound with need. She belonged to him and by all the gods in Roman creation, she would remain his... No. He couldn't do that. He had to tell her the truth before he made any claims on her.

He tore his mouth from hers.

She looked petulant and annoyed.

Ah, how he would enjoy taming her into pleasurable submission.

"Lyla," he whispered. "We must speak."

"I would much rather do this." She grasped his head between her hands and kissed the breath from his body.

He grabbed her arms, and pulled them down to her sides. "Listen to me, please."

"Yes, *dominus et deus*." She grinned.

He longed to haul her across his lap and spank her impertinent butt. He had no doubt she would enjoy it. So would he.

Time enough for that, but now, I must be truthful! "I want you to know that you are not a prisoner here."

She stilled. Then her face grew cloudy with doubt. "You've told me that before."

"You can leave any time. The book is your key to the portal that brought you here. By stroking that stone on the cover, you propel yourself backwards or forwards in time."

A corner of her mouth lifted. "Really?"

"Really."

"So, I could leave now, if I wished?"

His heart plummeted until it felt leaden in his chest. Guilt ate away at him, for he knew he didn't tell the entire truth. "Yes, if you so desired, you could leave." He continued in a rush, lest he lose his nerve, "But there are perils with time travel, and no guarantees that you will wind up back in your time."

She narrowed her eyes. "When we were in the book store, you told me you went back and visited your family. So that book took *you* here, to Ancient Rome."

"I've been lucky. My father wasn't."

"What do you mean?" She sat up and tossed her hair back over her shoulders.

He fingered the soft, silky strands, enjoying the sweet fragrance of the tiny flowers entwined in her locks. "I believe that my father pioneered time travelling. He discovered that all he had to do was stroke the 'magic gemma' imbedded in the cover of the book so he could travel back and forth between this era and the future. Then, for some reason, I believe he wound up in some other century. He may have tried to get back to my mother and me, and perhaps he did, because he brought the book back with him."

"But he didn't stay?"

Marcus ground his fist against his thigh. It was a while before he answered.

"Time travel is fraught with peril." He took a deep breath, and released it. "For all I know, he could have ended up in the Dark Ages, and died from the plague."

"But how could he have ended up there, if the book is the key to time travelling? Wouldn't he have taken the book with him?"

"I'm n-not sure." He looked away.

"Marcus, please tell me."

He gazed at her. Once more, his heart felt heavy, his shoulders sagging from the emotional weight he carried within him. It was time he faced the truth about his father.

"I think someone may have murdered him, when he came back to Rome."

"Why?"

"Perhaps, they desired the book—maybe the person who murdered him thought the book was worth a lot of coin because of the gems lining the cover."

She rested a hand on his cheek. "I'm sorry."

"Such are the risks men of daring take. My father was that kind of man. He latched onto a new idea, and anytime someone does that, they take a great chance."

She angled her head. "So are you," she said softly. "You are a man of daring." She frowned in thought. "But how did this time-travelling book come into existence?"

"The stone is the key. Books are not known here, in this period in history. My father must have brought the book back here from his travels forward. I think he embedded the stone in the cover, along with a myriad of other gems, to hide its real purpose." He pulled her towards him and rested his forehead against hers. "The other stones are rare gems and worth a great deal of money. Romans are greedy." His lips grazed her skin. He felt her shudder in response. "Now that I'm an adult I can see things more clearly. When I was younger, I just thought my father went away because he didn't like us, but now, I realise, that he didn't leave my mother and me—he was probably murdered. I just wish I knew who did it."

"They might have murdered him, but they never took the book. Why?"

"I think my father knew someone was after him, and he gave Decimus the book for safe keeping. Decimus hid it beneath the floor of my father's study. That's how I discovered it, you know. After my father left us, I remember walking into his room." He ran a hand through his hair then dropped that hand to his side. "I always hoped I would walk in and see my father there, sitting at his table, writing on a papyrus scroll. Anyway, I felt a loose floor tile, and when I lifted it, I discovered the book, and soon I figured out the power behind the 'magic gemma'. I was twenty years old when I started to time travel, and I've been doing it ever since."

She fingered the hair on his chest. He lifted her fingers and kissed them.

"So, I simply stroke that stone, and I can return to my time?"

"Yes. I will not stop you, ever." But he wanted to. He wanted to keep her here by his side, forever. He longed to take her on a sensual journey of her mind and body that would bind her to him always.

"Where is the book now?"

"I keep it in my bedchamber. Anytime you want, you may view it or...use it for its real purpose. To get home."

She bit down on her lower lip. He wanted to nip it, too.

Seconds went by. Perspiration lined his back while he waited for her to respond.

"I will go when I am ready," she told him. "And not before."

His heart beat wildly. "Are you ready now?"

She shook her head and smiled. "No."

That's all he needed to hear. His body, once tight with anxiety and tension, relaxed.

He stripped his tunic, ripping it over his chest and head, his dick so hard he thought it would burst. He needed to take her, and he needed to do it now, her affirmation that she wanted to stay, making his desire for her more potent. But if he didn't slow down, he'd spill himself before he was even inside her.

Damn her for making him want her so much! She had no idea the effect she wrought on his mind and body.

Sweat beaded on his upper lip. The little witch noticed. She leaned over and lapped it up with her tongue. It sent a jolt of sensual pleasure to his loins.

Okay, so he could fight fire with fire. He ran a finger down her breast, touching her tender little nipple. "Did you enjoy your time with your ornators?"

She blushed to the roots of her very pale hair. "How did you know? Did Eisha and Corinne tell you?"

He stretched out next to her, resting the side of his head in his palm. He ran a finger down her breast. "No one had to tell me, I knew all about it."

She narrowed her eyes. "How?"

"I watched."

Her face turned crimson.

"There are small viewing holes drilled into the walls. You just have to know where to find them."

"You wretch!" She tossed a pillow at him.

He laughed, ducking before the pillow reached its intended target—his head. He couldn't remember when he'd smiled and laughed so much. "Temper, my sweet." He chuckled.

He rose over her, brushing the entrance of her sex with his stiff cock. That's what her fiery disposition did to him; it made him horny as hell. *And damn her for choosing that as her 'safe' word.*

"So, you think that now that you watched me enjoying two women, you can have your wicked way with me?" She widened her legs, allowing him entrance. Then she ran a hand across his chest.

"I want to say something to you, in your language," she whispered against his mouth.

"Latin. That's what we speak here."

"How do I say…" She ran a hand down his chest. Her fingers dipped lower, where she grabbed his cock. "'You have a magnificent body'?"

"Vos a splendidus somes, Vinco."

"Oh," she sighed. "It sounds lovely." She hugged him tight.

"You say it now."

"Vos a splendidus somes."

"Ah," he ran a finger down her nose. "You left out a word."

She frowned. "What word did I miss?"

"Master," he hissed. "The word for 'master' in Latin is 'vinco.' Now, say it again," he commanded.

"Vos a splendidus somes , Vinco."

She ran the pad of her thumb across his cock.

Her words flowed over him, making him feel strong and powerful.

He reached under a pillow, withdrawing another condom. How he longed to feel his naked cock in her channel, but he wouldn't take that chance. He didn't want her to return to her time pregnant with his child.

He rode her slowly, sliding in and out, making sure to touch the tip of his cock to her clit. He wanted them to be in total communion, wanted every part of him to touch her.

He gathered her close and pumped into her.

"Master," she breathed. "*Vinco.*"

It was like beautiful, sweet music to his ears.

He took her until she cried, "Marcus!"

He froze. She had used his Roman name.

He rode her again, slowly at first, but her voice uttering his name echoed through his mind, making him want to burn through her like a fiery comet.

He had seen one in his youth. He always wondered if that marked the arrival of those strange beings his father claimed to have acquired that mysterious stone from, the one that could send a person into oblivion if they weren't careful.

Oddly enough, it didn't matter. For now, he had his own eternity in his arms.

She arched her back, digging her long nails into his hips.

He gritted his teeth. Sweat popped out on his brow. He kissed her mouth, positive that he had bruised her lips, such was his need for her.

He couldn't hold out anymore, pounding into her with such force so that she arched her back again. This time, she wrapped her legs around his back, her heels beating a rhythm on his back.

He spilled his seed into the condom, resting his forehead against hers. Worries swirled through his brain. He had no doubt that she would investigate that book and its magic stone. But he knew, in his heart of hearts, that he could never let her go.

That's why he never revealed the secret that would truly enable her to return to her time. Guaranteed.

* * * *

The next morning, Lyla woke alone. She stretched out her arm, her hand seeking the cushion she shared with Marcus.

Marcus.

He was no longer Mark, that, sexy, modern man she met in the bookstore. He was a noble Roman, a peer of his realm.

Marcus.

A slow smile spread across her face.

Master.

Her perfect alpha male.

Appia came with her breakfast. "Good morning, mistress."

"Good morning," Lyla murmured in response. No matter what Marcus told her, she still remained his prisoner, trapped by his glorious body and his potent, dominating allure.

What a sweet incarceration!

She glanced at Appia. "Where is Mar—I mean, where is the Master this morning?"

"He has gone out for a while, on business."

She wondered what 'business' he was up to. Acquiring more slaves? What would happen when he tired of using her? Lyla squashed that thought, but her anxiety grew. Would he give her back to Corvus? Maybe he'd allow Domitian to take her.

She pushed those thoughts aside, remembering his promise to protect her. She had to trust that he would do as he swore.

"Will you send me my ornators, please?"

Appia smiled and bowed. "Will there be anything else?"

"No, thank you." She watched Appia walk out.

While she ate, she pondered that story Marcus had told her last night. She could leave any time she wanted. All she had to do was use the power of that book and its magic stone.

It wasn't that she feared being a slave, his personal *lupa.*

She was afraid that she liked it too much.

* * * *

Later, Eisha and Corinne bathed and dressed her.

Lyla wore a long, white gown with a criss-cross bodice. The garment's daring cut revealed both her breasts. They styled her hair so that some lay piled in a curly mass atop her head, while the rest trailed down in waves. Tiny seed pearls and jewels adorned the fancy hairdo. Her lips and cheeks were reddened again with vegetable dye.

She gazed at her reflection, deciding that she resembled a cool, Roman woman of high rank, despite her slave status.

Finally, she slipped her feet into butter soft, strappy leather sandals.

In her time, she couldn't strut her stuff this way. She'd be arrested for indecency. Here, it was expected *and* accepted.

Decimus came for her. "I will take you on a tour of his Excellency's home." His eyes found her breasts. Decimus nodded in approval. "The master will be well pleased."

The notion that Marcus would be happy sent her clit throbbing with need. A tiny trickle of moisture seeped down her leg. She wished she could wear underwear.

"Something wrong?" The wily little man didn't miss a trick.

She angled her chin. "I wish to wear undergarments."

"His Excellency does not like women who wear the typical Roman undergarment, a *subligar and subligaculum*."

"Oh."

"He does not want your breasts bound, or your *valum* covered."

She lifted a brow, hoping she looked confident. "He wants me ready, willing, and able at any time, is that it?" The idea of submitting to Marcus whenever he wanted made her heart pound and her body react in frighteningly wanton way.

Decimus didn't speak for a few seconds. Then he smiled and bowed slightly. "Precisely."

She sighed. No use trying to get the upper hand with Decimus... Or his handsome master.

Decimus led her around Marcus' magnificent home. She'd seen very little, her early defiance distracting her.

He lived in grand splendour in the busy, bustling city of ancient Rome. There were outdoor pools and gardens built on his vast acreage. Wild animals roamed freely. She watched two zebras chase each other.

"I never dreamt Romans lived this way," she marvelled.

"Our master has a great interest in many things."

"Including slaves?"

Decimus stopped walking. He turned to face her. "Here, in this time, there is no, what our Master calls 'automation'. 'Machines', as he refers to them, do not do the needed work. We need slaves to do it."

"Slavery caused the downfall of the Roman empire," she reminded him.

"His Excellency has told me so." He stretched out his hand, indicating that they should walk again.

She fell into step beside him. "Doesn't that frighten you to know that?"

"I will be long dead when it happens."

"So, you don't care what happens to everyone else?" She raised a brow.

He clasped his hands together behind his back. "My master's travels through time are just that. A journey.

Nothing he does may stop anything that is bound to happen. He treats all people with great care and concern, knowing that it is the slaves who keep Rome afloat and in it's grandeur, so that at a time far into the future, people will be able to enjoy many Roman designs and devices. Like the wheel. We ancient Romans made the most use of it, for chariots, covered coaches and farm carts. We've also mastered mathematics in our architecture. The giant dome in the market is an example of angles and lines, and mathematical equations. It will be, according to our master, quite some time before the world will see such buildings again. But the necessary evil, slavery, is what brings it to life. My master knows this, so he treats us well."

She snorted. "If you're a slave, you remain a slave, just to serve the empire. You'd think your *master* would want to do something to eradicate it, knowing what the future holds."

"My master will do nothing to upset the time's delicate fabric, for if he did, many things in *your time* would not be as they are now. *You* could be living a much harder existence."

"Like what? What could possibly be so wrong with dissolving the right to own slaves?"

"As I stated earlier, the great architecture of the Roman empire would be lost, for slaves built it."

"We could do without a few Doric columns. After all, Roman architecture seems as though it relied on Greek architectural designs."

"The Greeks owned slaves, too. Who do you think built their homes and temples?"

She sighed. "It is a vicious cycle."

"It is the way of the world."

They ended up in the atrium.

"I will leave you here to ponder it all." Decimus bowed. "And remember, your wish is our command, and pleasure."

He left her sitting on a stone bench surrounding a fountain. She dipped her hand in the cool water, splashing some on her neck and arms.

Marcus' theories about not changing things be damned! If she stayed here with him, she'd be his slave forever. *Is that what I truly want?*

She got up and marched into the house and sought Marcus' bedchamber. She knocked on the door once, thinking he might have returned. When he didn't respond, she opened the door and peeked her head in.

It was empty, save for a few pieces of furniture. A wide, canopied bed sat against the far wall. For just a second, Lyla wished Marcus *were* here, so she could share that magnificent bed with him. *Fool! Concentrate on your task. Find that book...*

She walked over to a marble table. Scrolls lay strewn on its surface. Buried beneath them, she noticed the gold binding of the large tome she sought.

She pushed the scrolls aside. Her heart raced when she saw the book's cover. The hourglass-shaped gemstone winked at her while it sparkled in the light.

It begged for her touch. She could go back home now. Her fingers shook.

Do I really want to leave him?

Yes! Go, now, before it is too late.

She slid her fingers downward, stroking the gem's smooth surface. She sucked in a breath, waiting for the walls around her to melt away.

Nothing happened.

She stroked the stone again. She had been light-headed the last time.

She waited. Minutes went by but she remained where she was, her head clear, the room still and silent.

"Damn him!" She pounded a fist on the book cover.

A deep, familiar voice echoed through the room. "That is no way to treat a priceless heirloom."

She looked up to see Marcus standing in the doorway, his tall frame filling the entrance. He looked proud and masterful, his red toga strewn across his fine linen tunic. His wavy, dark hair styled in a close-cropped cut made his prominent nose stand out even more.

Unshed tears almost choked her. She held them back, prepared to do battle with him. "You liar. You insane man," she hissed. "But I must be just as sick to have believed your bullshit story about this book."

He walked into the room and slid the doors shut behind him. "Watch your tongue, Lyla."

She rounded the table and stood with him, toe to toe. "You told me I wasn't a prisoner, so I can act any way I damn well please."

His eyes sought her bared breasts.

Damn, but her traitorous body always got her in trouble. Her nipples pebbled when his hot look caressed her.

She took a step back.

"Your journey here is not yet complete."

"What sort of nonsense is that?"

"The book will not return you to your time unless you finish what you started here."

"What am I supposed to finish here in *this* time? Being your *lupa*?"

"Precisely."

I thought he was starting to care for me. Her shoulders slumped. A deep ache filled her heart. How could she have believed such foolishness from him?

Maybe it was the damned wine. It was probably tainted. She'd have believed anything he said or showed her if her mind was cloudy with a drug that stole her will.

"I won't sleep with you again," she said through clenched teeth. "Ever."

He let go of a deep sigh. "I will never force myself on you."

Tears burned her eyes when she tried to hold them back. A huge, shuddering sob escaped from her chest.

"Lyla." He took a step forward. "You need to understand. The book will let you know when you can leave."

"Oh yeah, right, sure. What does it do? Talk?" She rolled her eyes.

"In a way, yes. It does." He angled his head. "It contained a message for you before, remember? Back in the book store."

"Probably something *you* wrote."

"I can't write in that book. It wouldn't let me."

"Right. Uh, huh."

His face fell. "I wish with all my heart that I could do something to make you believe me."

She took in a calming breath, but it didn't slow her racing pulse. "Well, there isn't. So don't try." Her voice shook. One lone tear slipped from her eye. It travelled down her cheek.

He reached out and brushed it aside.

She whipped her head away, but not before the tip of his finger connected with her cheek. The contact made her body shudder.

"I should have told you the whole truth about that book, but I didn't want you to go." His face looked drawn and solemn. His shoulders slumped. "But now, I wish I did, because I'd rather do anything than disappoint you."

"Leave me alone," she bit out.

He inclined his head. "If that's what you wish."

"It is."

He turned around and walked towards the door.

Damn it, why didn't he stay and argue with her? Why did he surrender? What vexed her more was that she still wanted to give in to *him*.

Anger bloomed inside her. She reached for a metal pitcher filled with water. She hurled it at his head, barely missing him. The container crashed against the door and fell on the floor, the liquid splashing Marcus' legs.

He looked down at his wet sandals. Then he turned around slowly.

She swore in that minute that his taut, angry look matched hers. Her chest heaved. She ran towards him, intent on scratching his face with her nails.

Before she could utter any protest, he scooped her up and dumped her on the bed. She scooted away from him, but he possessed greater speed. He reached for her, grabbing her legs.

She shrieked in frustration and anger. Oh, if she could find something to hit him with!

"Calm down," he told her. Heaving his body over hers, he stretched her arms upwards, holding both wrists in one of his hands. His weight settled across her, pinning her body to the bed.

"Get off—"

He leant down and silenced her with his lips. The heat of his mouth burned through her while he crushed her lips in a rough, commanding kiss. He released her wrists. Instinctively, her arms twined around his neck.

She loved his hot, branding kiss. And hated him for making her feel that way.

When he finished plundering her mouth, he did the same with her breasts, his mouth wreaking havoc on her nipples. That sweet throbbing started between her legs.

She knew she should stop him. Marcus had released her arms so she could pummel him at any time. She could also use her 'safe' word.

She didn't want to. She wanted the sweet torture to go on and on.

He hiked up her gown and placed his hand on the juncture between her thighs. Her back arched when he rubbed her clit with the tip of his index finger.

"I am a Roman, alpha male," he whispered in her ear, his voice gruff and powerful. "It is what you want, Lyla. The one thing you crave from me is domination."

She whimpered in protest.

"I command you to come." His voice held wicked, deep notes.

She tried to hold back, just to spite him.

"You will be punished if you don't do as I say." He kept rubbing her clit.

Punishment. The word alone sent her into a tailspin of sensual need. He knew the exact sensual button to push to send her over the edge.

She didn't want to give in, but the more he massaged her labia, the more her body betrayed her. Finally, she cried out her pleasure, her back arching upwards so that her breasts shoved into his mouth again. He took each one while she came, heightening her release even more.

She placed her hands around his back, digging her nails into his flesh.

He didn't say anything; it was like he didn't even feel it. Instead, he captured her mouth again with his lips.

"It is the only way I know to silence you." He grinned. "That," he stroked the hair from her face that lay across her cheeks in damp tendrils, "and this." He kissed her breasts again, and laid a hand between her thighs.

She clamped them shut, finally coming to her senses. If she let the lying bastard have his way again, she'd lose all control. "Leave me alone."

He rose on his elbows and looked down at her, confusion lining his face.

She enjoyed that he seemed perplexed. It shifted the power balance into her court.

She uttered the one word she knew that would place the control back in her hands. "Horny." Her voice was flat and devoid of emotion.

He nodded, lifting his weight from her.

Her eyes filled with tears. Damn him. Why did he have to act with honour now? "I won't believe your stupid lies anymore and I won't be your slave."

He pointed his index finger at her. "And when *you* are ready to accept the truth about yourself, and that book, let me know." He did as she bade, leaving her to sulk on the bed.

Lyla stayed there until her heartbeat slowed to a normal rhythm.

She got up and straightened her gown and hair, trying to make herself look presentable. That sweet ache built in her clit again.

She collapsed on the bed, shutting her eyes, trying to blot out the memory of Marcus' hand between her legs.

She wanted it there. She wanted *him* there. She needed his huge cock inside her. Again and again, and again…

She suddenly realised her need for Marcus far outweighed her desire to go home. It hurt more to face that fact than when Corvus had chained her to that cage in his prison, causing her physical pain.

She glanced at her wrists, the bruising barely visible. Marcus had seen to it that she healed. He'd also seen to her other needs. Mostly, her need for *him*.

She heard a rustling sound. She sat up, trying to judge where the odd noise came from.

Marcus' writing table.

Her eyes widened. She saw the strange old book open of its own accord. A breeze lifted the pages, but no air swirled around her.

Slowly, she rose from his bed, and walked towards the tome. Page after page unfurled, as though lifted by some unseen hand.

She glanced out the window, thinking that a breeze came from there, but the air remained still. "It's another trick," she muttered.

But he had left the room. He couldn't possibly make that book move like that, unless…

She glanced upwards thinking an air vent must be overhead but she felt no breeze.

The pages stopped fluttering. The book lay open, revealing the yellowed pages. She moved closer and reached for the tome, turning it so she could read.

Your journey is not complete,
It has just begun.
You will learn much more,
Before you can return home.

Snap! She closed the book, not believing the words. Mark must have placed them there. But just the same, she glanced around, hoping no one could see.

She rubbed the gemma until her fingers burned from the friction. Nothing happened.

Frustration filled her, she wanted to pound on the book's cover until her hands became raw.

Why do I persist in believing such nonsense? Have I truly gone mad?

Something shiny caught her eye. A metal object lay beneath the scrolls on Marcus' desk. A gold band peeked out from beneath the papyrus rolls.

Her watch! She looked at the timepiece. The hands turned rhythmically, the big one marking down the seconds. Then, both hands spun around the face of the watch. It made her dizzy. She gripped the table for support. Then, everything stopped.

She didn't know how long she stood there, expecting something to happen.

The walls didn't melt away. She didn't slip into that tunnel. She wasn't propelled forwards in time, but remained exactly where she was.

She looked at the watch again. The hands were still. She banged the watch on the table, but the hands wouldn't budge.

It was as though she had got into her car and started it but when she placed her foot on the gas pedal, the car wouldn't move.

Time as she knew it, remained in neutral. So, did she.

She sank to her knees and wrapped her arms around her waist, hugging them to her body.

She couldn't stop shaking.

You will learn much more, before you can return home.

The words swirled through her mind. And heart.

Home, she always heard, was where your heart lay.

A strange feeling of detachment came over her. Or maybe, it was the realisation that her modern day existence didn't seem like home.

And probably never was.

Chapter Ten

Sometime later, Lyla woke to the sound of a low moan.

She opened her eyes to total darkness and stretched out her legs, her cramped muscles resisting the movement. Pain shot through her thighs.

How long have I been lying on the floor? She gazed around her, allowing her eyes to adjust to the dark.

A cry sounded through the night. When she realised from where it came, she turned her head to the right. From the room next door, she heard a woman shout, *"Haud!"*

Another raised voice drifted to her ears. A man's. It sounded like Marcus.

Her pulse raced. Was he harming some poor woman? A slave? Maybe Eisha or Corinne?

She shook her head to clear it of her crazy thoughts. It didn't make sense. Why would he hurt them after he had gone to the trouble of rescuing them from Corvus?

She remembered Marcus' statement about the rooms having small peepholes in them, so she rose to her feet and climbed onto the bed. Perhaps his bedroom contained a tiny viewing device...

She ran her fingers over the wall, touching something slightly raised and round. She pressed her eye against it and discovered she had a clear view to another room.

Her breath caught in her chest. She blinked once, not quite believing what she saw...a collection of what appeared to be whips and crops, each mounted on a wall. The lashes were different shapes and sizes. One resembled a leather strap; another was made from twisted parchment thongs.

Lyla couldn't tear her eyes away from the deadliest looking whip constructed of long lashes and spiked at the ends with metal points. Lyla's gaze soon beheld another sight.

Appia stood in the centre of the room, her head bowed. Marcus' tall frame filled the space before her. He raised her chin with his palm, speaking rapidly in Latin.

The young girl quaked. Her entire body shook, from head to toe. Then she answered him.

Marcus' face grew stormy. Appia bowed her head. A long silence greeted Lyla. Then Marcus spoke again.

He paced before Appia. He spoke, his tone angry. His voice boomed throughout the room

Appia wrung her hands, her response quick. Her voice shook when she addressed him.

He raised her chin, and uttered a command. She sank back on her heels.

He said something else, his tone questioning. Appia bit her lower lip. She answered, but from the sound of Marcus' voice, it appeared as though he did not like what she said.

Appia rose to her feet and stood before him.

He grabbed a chair then raised his voice. It sounded as if he issued a command.

Appia pulled up her tunic with shaking hands, baring herself from the waist down.

Lyla's heart pounded. She swore she could hear each racing beat, thought that they could hear it, too.

Again Marcus barked out what sounded like an order. Appia exposed her naked ass to Marcus.

He walked over to where the whips and crops were positioned on the wall. He studied them for a few seconds then chose the leather strap.

He said the word *feruala* several times. Lyla wondered if that's what he called the leather strap in his hand.

He didn't give Appia a warning. He let the long piece of leather fly through the air. It landed on Appia's backside, the sound of it hitting her flesh making a loud, 'crack'.

Lyla's mouth grew dry while sweat beads formed on her back. Several trickled down, soaking her gown. She hid her face in her hands, not wanting to watch, yet, some perverse little part of her did.

She watched as Appia's lashing with the whip continued.

Her cunt throbbed. She stroked herself there, between her legs, knowing that Marcus couldn't see. A wicked, yet shameful feeling overcame her.

The more Marcus spanked Appia with the ferula, the redder the girl's ass became.

Lyla moaned when her fingers brought her the needed release she sought from the salacious spectacle she viewed through the peephole.

For just a second, Marcus stopped his punishment. He turned his head in her direction.

Lyla scooted back down in his bed, making herself into a tight ball.

Then she heard the sound of the leather against Appia's bottom, wishing it were *she* who received punishment. She spread her legs and rubbed her tender clit, bringing release to her throbbing body once again.

Marcus would never know how much she enjoyed viewing that scene. The imp inside her danced, but then it stopped when guilt reared its ugly head.

She had to find out why Appia was being punished. Perhaps she'd placed herself in danger again.

She'd speak to Appia and discover the truth, and maybe, just maybe…

Receive *her* heart's desire from Marcus, as well.

* * * *

The following day, Lyla met Appia on the way to the bath.

Appia looked beautiful, her dark hair swept upwards into a tight bun with several braids wound together. Tendrils of dark hair escaped, curling down the sides of her face. Her silk gown's pale rose colour accentuated Appia's smooth, olive-toned skin. She approached Lyla, her steps measured, for it seemed that when she walked, it pained her.

Lyla could imagine. Her bottom tingled in response, despite her efforts to control her reaction. "You look lovely," she told Appia, angling her head. "Are you dressed for some a special occasion?"

Appia's lovely, reddened lips split into a wide smile. "Yes." She bowed her head. "I am to meet my future husband today."

"Appia, please don't say you're going through with that sham of a marriage to Marcus' friend." She gripped the young girl's shoulders.

Appia removed herself from Lyla's hold. "That's exactly what I'm doing." She raised her chin.

Lyla bit down on her lower lip. While she hated Marcus' plan for Appia to wed his friend, she wondered if he told the girl about reuniting with her family. It was a chance for Appia to escape servitude, and be with her people again.

A twinge of jealousy touched Lyla's heart. She did not have any family back home who gave two shits about her.

Despite the spanking Marcus administered, he still seemed to care a great deal about Appia's happiness, about her reuniting with her family.

Suddenly, Lyla didn't want to betray his confidence because of her own bitterness. But she couldn't accept that this sweet, pretty girl would marry a stranger, solely based on Marcus' word.

Lyla's shoulders slumped. This wasn't the modern world, but ancient Rome. Things like this probably happened all the time.

But damn! Lyla's hand knotted into a fist at her side. If Appia gave her the slightest indication that she wasn't happy, Lyla would endure the worst beating imaginable to stop this archaic bullshit.

"Lyla, I want you to know that I am very pleased about all this." Appia's smile lit her entire face, but then it drooped just a bit. "Except, that I will miss this household, and everyone in it." She took Lyla's hand in her own and gave it a gentle squeeze. "I have experienced great kindness here, and, well, forgiveness."

"What do you mean?"

"The master is still allowing me to meet his friend, Cletus. We will all share a meal, so I can get acquainted with my future." She smiled. "I mean, my future husband."

"But why do you say, the master is still allowing it to happen? Did you do something that made him change his mind?"

She thought of that spanking Marcus gave Appia.

Appia's eyes darted around then drew Lyla off to the side. She raised her gown, revealing her bottom, now tinged a deep pink shade.

Lyla licked her lips. "Wh-what happened?"

Appia spoke almost in a whisper. "I stole from the master."

"Oh, Appia, why? For what reason?"

"I thought about what you said to me when you first got here. About making choices for my future. I figured if I could steal some gold cups and sell them, that I might escape my fate."

Lyla sighed. "That's not what I meant. I meant that you should voice how you feel about things. That you should have a say in your life."

"I understand that all now, but at the time, I didn't."

"So I guess Marcus found out about you stealing from him?"

"Yes, he did. I felt so bad about it, that I confessed all to the master, and when he told me about the plans he had for me to meet Cletus, and that I would see my family again…"

Lyla's eyes widened. "He told you about that?"

"Yes, and I was so ashamed about what I'd done. About taking those cups from him."

Lyla gripped her shoulders again. "Do you realise Marcus could have had you killed for stealing from him?"

A shudder tore through Appia. "Yes, I do. He told me so, too."

"Appia, you should have told me what you planned to do. Marcus confided in me about you reuniting with your family." She shook her head. "I could have prevented this."

"No, Lyla. You are not to blame."

"Yes, I am. I should have kept my big mouth shut when I first got here."

"It is my own fault. I thought that stealing would somehow allow me to buy my way out of everything."

"It just made it worse for you." Lyla could barely meet Appia's gaze.

"Yes, it did."

"And that's why Marcus be—I mean, punished you?"

"Well." Appia's face reddened. "That's not the only reason."

Lyla frowned. "What then?"

"I begged him to forgive me for taking what belonged to him."

Lyla recalled how Appia got on her knees before Marcus.

"Did he?"

"Yes."

Lyla shook her head. "Then why did he punish you anyway?"

"Because he asked me who filled my head with doubts about the marriage."

Uh, oh... "D-did you tell him that it was me who did that?"

Appia shook her head. "No."

"But why?"

"Perhaps because I knew how unhappy you were when you first came here, how you longed to escape. I remembered feeling that way once, too, when I first arrived in the master's house. I knew you didn't mean what you said, and well, whatever I chose to believe, the decision I made to steal from the master was mine alone. You didn't aide me in that."

Lyla slumped against the wall. "But I did say all that about making your own choices."

Appia placed a hand on Lyla's arm. "It doesn't matter now. What matters is that the Master forgave me, and I can still meet Cletus. As it turns out, the Master told me that nothing will happen unless I'm truly in agreement with it."

Trust Marcus to turn the tables on her! Here she thought he'd commanded Appia to marry his friend.

Suddenly, Lyla longed to be forgiven for her role in messing everything up for this young girl. She couldn't allow Appia to take the rap for something that *she'd* instigated. She didn't know how to approach Marcus and ask for chastisement...or forgiveness.

Besides, she was still angry with him for his lies. She didn't want anything to do with him, or did she? How would she get what she truly deserved and needed from him?

Lyla looked down at Appia's hand. It felt soft and smooth, her skin fragrant with a fruity, floral scent. Cletus would have to be crazy not to fall instantly in love with her. Envy crept into her heart, making her feel small and bitter.

How she wished so many times for the same thing for herself — for a man to fall head over heels in love with her.

Maybe, as she had thought once before, nothing really had changed in a couple of thousand years.

Lyla returned Appia's grin. "Your future is your husband. He will fall madly in love with you."

Appia gave a slight bow. "Thank you, mistress." She walked away, stopping for a second. Turning her head, she uttered in a hushed voice, "I wish the same for you, too."

Lyla's eyes stung. She choked on tears while she made her way to the bath, not bothering to summon her ornators. She desired solitude, needing to lick her secret emotional wounds in private.

When she entered the baths, she discovered Marcus there. He swam in the pool, diving headfirst into the fragrant, steamy water. When he surfaced, he shook his dark head, droplets of water spraying into the air.

She was about to leave when he called out to her.

"Join me, Lyla." He swam to the ledge. His voice dipped an octave. "I would be your ornator and wash you."

She angled her chin. "No, thank you."

"You are still angry with me."

She folded her arms across her breasts. "I'm always angry with people who lie to me."

"And I am very sorry for it, but Lyla, I..."

"What?" Her heart raced.

"I just didn't want you to leave."

She blinked once, not quite registering what she heard.

"Can you forgive me for being selfish? For wanting you to stay?"

He wanted her... *When was the last time anyone desired me? Oh, but I want so much more from you, Marcus.*

How could she forgive him, when she couldn't absolve herself for causing Appia's lashing? She couldn't assuage her culpability, choosing to hold onto her anger for Marcus. It was a much safer emotion to deal with.

He rested his forearms on the ledge. Then he placed his chin atop his hands.

"Time travelling isn't an entitlement, you must earn it, discovering new and wonderful things about yourself. That's why that gemma didn't release you and propel you forwards, to your own time."

"I wish you'd stop talking about that, for I don't believe a word."

"I think you do." His dark eyes bored into hers.

"I *know* that I hate you. That is something I've *discovered*."

His dark eyes flashed. "Now, who's the liar?" He frowned, glancing at her chest. "Why do you not display your magnificent breasts?"

Her boldness returned. She shoved down her dress, revealing her naked chest. "There. Happy now?" She quickly pushed her gown upwards, giving him a smug look.

He shook his head, sadness lining his face. "I would rather you argue with me."

"But I'm supposed to obey your every command, aren't I?"

He grinned. "Ah. That's better."

"What?" She frowned.

"You just debated with me." He chuckled. "It always amazes me how easily I can draw you in."

She walked over to the pool, sticking her foot in the water. She raised her toes high in the air, pushing water into his face.

He growled low in his throat then grasped her around the ankle. She lost her balance and toppled over into the pool. She came up sputtering.

"You don't play fair!" She heaved her body over to the side, her wet garment weighing her down.

"That wasn't nice to splash water in your master's face."

She turned around and hit the water's surface with her hand, making a wide arc. In the next instant, a huge wave hit Marcus in the face. She scrambled from the pool before he could catch her. Her pulse raced with delight. This is what she loved best, to get back at him.

She hoped he would punish her for it. And for what she did to Appia.

His dark, smouldering look sent a pleasant zing through her body. "You got away with that, my sweet, but you won't always."

* * * *

She waited in her room, expecting Marcus to come storming in. She hoped he would drag her to that room filled with whips.

Time passed, but when Marcus didn't show, she left her room, encountering Decimus in the hallway. "Where is the master?" she asked, hoping she didn't sound too eager.

"He is still entertaining his friend and Appia."

"Oh." She chewed on her lower lip, hoping she hid her disappointment. Marcus' damned appointment with his friend was more important than her. Why couldn't he just leave Appia alone with Cletus? Did Marcus have to be there, as well?

Decimus seemed to read her mind. "His Excellency must make sure that Cletus and he come to an agreement on

Appia's dowry. A portion will be placed in her hands, should she decide this marriage is not for her. Cletus wants a willing bride, and well, they both want Appia's happiness."

"How positively gothic, to be speaking of a dowry." She rolled her eyes, but inside, her emotions did battle.

Trust Marcus to ensure that one of his people remained happy. His damned friend sounded like a good man, too. *How can I be angry with him for that?*

"Pardon me?" Decimus cupped his palm around his earlobe. "I'm not sure I heard you correctly. What is 'gotic'?"

"Gothic," she corrected.

"Gotik."

"It is pronounced with a 'th' not just a —" She sighed. "Just forget it."

"It shall be." He grinned.

She walked away in a huff but an idea took root in her mind.

Marcus entertained his friend and Appia. When he finished, she could speak to him about her punishment. Her palms grew damp at the thought.

Damn, why did she have to be honest with him, when he hadn't been the least bit honest with her? She shook her head, realising she lied to herself again.

His actions sprang from a selfish desire to keep her here. He owned up to his mistake. Now, she'd have to come to terms with hers.

The first had to do with Appia. The second was that she desired Marcus. She couldn't deny it any longer. She wanted him to make love to her the minute she saw him in the bookstore. She desired his complete domination.

As a motivator of people, she made others see just how messed up their lives were so they could make them better, but she'd never faced her personal chaos. Now, she had to.

It may not get her out of this godforsaken ancient land, but it would make her stronger. She'd need all her strength to deal with Marcus.

If she could just sneak into that 'punishment room' without Marcus knowing, she could decide which one he should use on her.

She glanced around to see that Decimus had left the hallway. Quietly, she made her way towards that wonderful little room filled with her heart's desire. She turned the knob on the door. It opened without hesitation.

She entered, sliding the doors shut behind her. She had to hurry, lest someone find her. The door possessed no lock, so if someone were to come in and see what she was up to, she'd be...

Punished.

A smiled spread across her face. Marcus would whip her bottom into submission.

Her pussy beat in time to her racing heart. Lyla raised her gown, tucking the hem into the band at her waist.

She walked over to the wall where the whips lay mounted in their holders and grabbed the lash made of twisted parchment thongs. Strange letters appeared etched into the handle.

She peered at it and read aloud, "*Scutica.*"

Glancing around, she noticed that the long, leather piece had writing burned into it. "*Ferula,*" she read. She had been correct in guessing that when Marcus used that word, 'ferula', it had been this whip.

Pleasure made her lips spread in a wide grin. Trust Marcus to name and label his chastisement devices.

Bending over a chair, she reached behind her, applying the scutica to her bare ass. It didn't give her the same satisfaction as watching Appia's punishment. She beat her ass harder, hoping to bring on release, but nothing happened.

She tossed the whip across the room, plunking her backside onto the chair.

If Marcus were here, she'd tearfully lay her transgression at his feet, and beg him to punish her. His use of the whip on her ass would release all her pent up anger, frustration, and shame.

She spread her legs and rubbed her cunt until she was almost raw.

Damn Marcus, and her need for *his* touch be damned, as well.

She had turned the tables, thinking she could mete out her own punishment but this time; she had turned them on herself.

* * * *

Marcus left Cletus and Appia in the atrium to give them some time alone. Cletus and he had been friends since childhood. He could trust him implicitly.

Besides, he missed Lyla. He wished fervently that she would have put her anger aside and joined them. He was a fool to think that she would.

After his blunder—his lie—she would never forgive him. He had been selfish enough to think that she wanted him as much as he desired her. He'd been an even bigger fool to think that she also wanted his total domination.

She may possess a wild, untamed side, but she didn't want *him*.

Somehow, he had to figure out another way to get her back to her own time, where she would be happy.

A tremor coursed through him when he realised that her happiness suddenly mattered more than what he wanted from her. Sweat trickled down his chest when he thought about it.

He walked from the atrium into his house, choosing to go into his bedchamber. Perhaps if he rested just a bit, and dreamt about her, she'd materialise like a goddess…

If that were to happen, he'd go to the temple and worship every single Roman god and goddess forever.

He unfastened his toga, swirling it away from his shoulders. He tossed it onto a chair. That's when he heard a cracking sound, as if a whip lashed against flesh.

He pressed his ear against the wall. He hadn't commanded anyone to be punished, and if he did, he would be doing it himself.

Marcus found the peephole. He glanced at the scene before him, his eyes growing wide.

Lyla bent her body over a chair, much in the same fashion as Appia had done when she received her chastisement except that Lyla tried to mete it out on her own body.

He grinned at the spectacle she made, her naked ass fully on display. And she had no idea he watched!

His cock grew stiff with need when she plunked her body down onto the chair and spread her legs wide. Slowly, she stroked her fingers across her labia.

He sat back on his heels and pondered her actions. Already, he owed her a spanking for splashing him in the pool, and now, she went against his command not to pleasure herself except when *he* ordered it.

He watched her frustration mount. She needed, as well as *wanted*, a sound beating on her ass.

She stopped stroking herself, dropping her head into her hands.

He smiled to himself, knowing that what she did had not satisfied her. At the same time, he filled with the need to soothe, and he wanted to drill her with his cock.

Domination rose within him.

Why did she want a spanking? Was it just some kinky need? In his mind, he examined the reasons. She snuck into his punishment room without his permission, and that alone would merit her chastisement.

Then again, how did she know about the room? Had Decimus showed it to her?

No, he shook his head. He'd told Decimus not to.

Marcus drew his eye away from the peephole, his mind a jumble of thoughts, his cock so hard he thought he would spill his seed right there. It pounded with need.

He couldn't *wait* to give Lyla what she truly desired...and deserved.

Chapter Eleven

Lyla had just about made it back to her room when two male slaves came for her. Tiny flutters tickled her abdomen, as if moths beat their wings inside her.

They escorted her to Marcus' bedchamber. When she entered, she found him sitting behind his writing table. At first, he didn't acknowledge her presence. He didn't say anything at all. Head bent, he continued to write, the stylus scratching on the rough papyrus.

It grated on her nerves.

Then he glanced upwards, regarding her much like a cat would a mouse. Her body tingled with alarm, yet her clit throbbed, too.

He said something to the two slaves. They bowed and exited, leaving Lyla alone with him. The door slid behind them with a loud and final sounding click.

Marcus leant back in the chair, his posture casual, but she sensed a coiled tension in him. The air in the room grew thick with it.

"What do you want?" she asked, her tone sharper than she'd intended, but damn, he made her so angry when he ignored her.

He raised a brow.

She rolled her eyes. "Master," she hissed. "What is your pleasure?" She drew out the last word.

He crooked his index finger. "Come here."

She angled her chin, hoping her defensive posture would hide her eagerness and fear of the unknown. It always seemed as though her emotions battled inside her, making her burn for Marcus' touch.

She took two, small steps forward.

"Closer."

She inched towards him, bringing her directly to his writing table.

"I've realised that I've made a big mistake with you," he told her, his voice deep.

She lifted her chin even higher. Better to keep a haughty distance between them. "It's about time you came to your senses, but if you're thinking an apology will do you're—"

"That wasn't my intention."

"Right. You've tried apologising already. Now just get me the hell away from this place."

"It is not in my power to do so."

"So, we're back to that…the book and that crazy story about the gemstone."

"The ability to return to your time is within you."

"Then I guess I'll just have to click my heels together to get me back to Oz."

"You're—what?" He scowled.

"Forget it." Exasperated, she let go of a long-suffering sigh. "So, you made a mistake in regard to me. Fine." She wiggled her fingers at him. "I'll be seeing you." She turned to leave.

"Subsisto!"

She hesitated for just a second because she didn't understand the Latin word, but when she turned around, she collided with his chest. Her nose bumped it. Her gaze travelled upwards until she stared into his face, drawn into tight lines.

His anger simmered just below the surface. "I didn't say you could leave."

"All right, make it quick, *Master*. I don't have all day." Damn, but she couldn't let him seduce her with his honeyed words and lies.

"My mistake has been allowing you the upper hand."

"Considering I'm your lupa, that's pretty hard for me to do, isn't it?"

"You're a slave in your own mind, Lyla. Until you break free, you'll always be a slave, mostly to your own brand of lies."

Fear snaked down her back, making it tingle. She hated that he was always so damned on target.

"You provide endless fascination." He angled his head, regarding her as if she were a bug under a microscope. "You are a wonderful motivator, I've seen that firsthand. You're someone who helps others turn their lives around, but you can't do the same thing for yourself."

"I've had enough." Her voice shook.

His voice deepened. "Not nearly, my sweet. You have a long list of wrongdoings that you must come to terms with."

Her heart raced. "Like what?" She frowned, thinking what he might know. "I suppose Decimus told you about my attempt to esca—"

His mouth kicked up. "Since you bring it up, let me just say that your failed plans to run away have turned my household upside down, as well as placing yourself in danger."

"It's a captive's responsibility to try and free herself."

"And I've told you, you're not a prisoner."

"Look, we can go 'round and 'round this, but it's going to get us nowhere. So why not just tell me all the bad things I've done?" She swiped her damp palms against her gown.

Had Appia mentioned anything to him?

"While I've kept that list right up here," he tapped his temple with his index finger, "it will be interesting to see it clearly, when we both write everything down."

"Write *what* down?"

"Your transgressions." His voice dipped an octave.

"Fine. Let's get to it." She walked over to his writing desk.

He brought a chair over for her. She plunked her bottom into the seat.

He shoved a small papyrus scroll at her and handed her a stylus. "Write. Then we'll compare our notes."

She shoved the papyrus aside, suddenly afraid. "Th-this is crazy."

"But very necessary." He shoved it back.

"Why?"

"You'll see."

Her body tingled in response, curiosity heightening her anticipation.

She unrolled the papyrus and wrote across it with the stylus. She handed both things back to Marcus.

He raised a brow. "You're done?"

"Yup."

He snatched the papyrus from her outstretched hands and read, "This sucks." He tossed it down onto the table.

She sat back in the chair, a smug smile spreading across her face.

"I'm disappointed in you, Lyla."

"Well, good. Maybe it's about time someone did that to you."

"I don't care about anyone else, just you."

"Well, I was very *sincere* in that I truly do think this entire bullshit thing sucks." She lied, for she had longed to pour her heart out on that papyrus and tell him everything that happened between her and Appia...and what she really wanted from him. But that would mean the power balance lay in his court. She wasn't sure she was ready to surrender—yet.

He regarded her thoughtfully. "Care to hear my list?"

She slumped in the chair. Her sarcasm didn't seem to scratch his tough, outer shell. "Go ahead," she mumbled. "Let's hear them."

What if Appia had broken down and told Marcus the truth? That it was Lyla who had whispered all those negative things in her ear about Cletus? Marcus would be pissed that she defamed his friend.

Is this Marcus' way of making me sweat it out? She bit down hard on her lower lip to stop it from quivering.

"Something wrong?"

"No!"

He raised a brow.

"Just read your damned list."

That brow rose higher.

"Master. Please read your list."

"All right. Number one—you use foul language. It undermines my authority with my household."

"Like they understand what *I* say. I don't speak Latin."

"Decimus and Appia understand it." Her face heated when he uttered Appia's name. "And my people can detect your tone and attitude. Two—your sarcasm makes it impossible to get to know the real you."

That took the breath from her body.

"It is something I'm dying to do, Lyla, to get to know the real you, but you prevent it at every turn."

That's because every man I've ever known before you hurt me. My own father didn't like me...

He read again. "Three—you don't want to change. While your circumstances have been precarious, you still react the same way."

She shot up from the chair. "How can you say that?" She placed her hands on the desk, anger making her shake. "When I was in Corvus' prison, I hung onto every shred of fight in me."

"While I admire that in you greatly, I just wish you wouldn't battle *me* that way, too."

"You said you liked that I always argue. Now you're singing a different tune?" She shook her head. "Why don't you make up your mind?"

He grinned.

"Why are you smiling?"

"That's better," he murmured. "At least you still want to debate."

Why do I always fall into his trap?

"Four—when I tried to make amends, you splashed me in the pool."

She held up a hand, palm out. "Wait a minute. *That* ticked you off?"

"What?"

"That I splashed you. In the pool."

He took a deep breath and let it out. "Yes, it *ticked me off*." He scowled. "You undermined my authority with the eunuchs. It shows no respect for your master."

"You lied to me, Marcus, and made up a ridiculous story about the book. *That's why* I splashed you." Tears threatened, but she held them back.

"That book really *is* your ticket away from here if you want it to be, Lyla. You just refuse to believe it because it won't do what you want it to do, when you want it to." He settled his hip on the table's corner and folded his arms across his chest.

Lyla swiped her hands on her thighs. "So, what now?" Her pulse sped up when he didn't speak.

"You're going to be punished."

Yes!

He walked over to the bed and sat down on it. "Come here." He patted his thighs. "Raise your gown, and lay yourself across my legs."

Whoa. She looked around. *Wasn't he going to use a whip?*

He lifted a brow. "Are you afraid?"

"Just, I mean, are you going to *spank* me?"

"Precisely." He softened his tone. "It will be over soon."

It sounds like he just wants to be done with me.

"Let's get this over with." He motioned with his hand.

Yup. She walked over to him, taking one small step at a time. A part of her craved this yet, something inside her rebelled. *This is not my heart's desire.*

"Turn around."

She did.

He lifted her gown, tucking the hem inside the waistband. Cool air swirled across her backside. It made it tingle.

He grabbed her upper arm. "Walk backwards, towards me."

She took a few steps.

"Place yourself over my lap."

Lyla sucked in a breath then bent over his thighs.

He placed a hand on her lower back, using just enough pressure so she couldn't move.

The first smack came without warning, his wide, flat palm landing directly on her butt cheeks. She cried out when the second one came, his hand enflaming her backside, and her loins.

He rained more slaps on her bottom. Her eyes filled with tears.

It wasn't so much from the pain; it was because the hand spanking was too sensual, too erotic, too…intimate. While his palm hit its intended target, it was off course as far as her emotions were concerned. She wanted, no *needed* more.

He gave her a warning. "You're receiving three more swats, Lyla. Then it will be done."

Her ass turned warm and tingly. It didn't hurt as much as it was supposed to. "Horny!" she cried.

She looked back to see his hand rise mid-air. He dropped it, and lifted the one he held on her lower back.

Lyla fell to the ground, her face awash with tears.

"No more." He reached for her, pulling her up to stand before him. He wiped the tears from her eyes with the pads of his thumbs. "No more, my sweet. I promise."

My sweet!

She wasn't sweet. She wasn't his. She'd never be that, unless she told him the truth. About Appia, and about what she really needed.

She wanted him to love her for what she was. A kinky bitch that adored those whips in his punishment room. She wanted real pain and chastisement, not a weak spanking that even he seemed loathed to administer.

Her feelings tangled up inside. She didn't know if she loved that kinky aspect of herself. How could she expect him to?

He tried to draw her into his embrace, but Lyla stopped him. "Why did you do that?" She swiped tears from her eyes, but she couldn't stem their flow.

He frowned. "It was your punishment. Surely, you understand that."

"Punishment? You call that *punishment?*"

Marcus turned her slightly so that she could view her pink bottom in the mirror. "I'd say it was." His frown deepened. "Unless you'd like to feel the flat of my hand again."

She scooted away from him and shoved her dress down to the floor. Lyla couldn't stand there and argue with him with her ass on display.

He ran a hand through his hair, his face filled with frustration. "What do you want from me, Lyla?" He spread his arms wide. "I can't guess anymore."

She raised her chin. "I want to be able to tell you the truth."

"*That* would be a refreshing change."

"Now who's being sarcastic?"

"I've learnt it from the *Master.*" He gave her a mock bow.

Her chest heaved. "You're not worth it." She turned on her heel to leave.

He pulled her back until she stood flush against his body. He placed his arms around her waist. Brushing back damp hair that stuck to her cheeks, he whispered, "Tell me."

She turned to face him. Tears shot from her eyes, landing on his red toga. They made dark stains in the fabric.

He looked down on them then raised his eyes to her. "Lyla, just say it, damn it. I can't bear this."

"*I* was the one who told Appia all that stuff about freedom and not being shackled to some man you chose for her." She wished a giant hole would rise up from the floor and swallow her.

He scrubbed a hand over his face then dropped that hand to his side. "Appia wouldn't reveal the person's name."

"It was I."

He nodded. "Fine. You told me and you received chastisement. You got what you wanted — and deserved."

She just looked at him, feeling as if a heavy weight lay on her chest. "Oh, Marcus, you foolish man." She wanted to cry all over again. "Maybe it is what I deserved, but it was *not* what I desired."

"So I'm to blame for spanking you, even though it was *you* who filled Appia's head with all those lies about my best friend?"

"No, I'm responsible for that."

"Then what's the problem, Lyla?"

"You took the easy way out." She shook her head. "And you did because you're afraid. You give me a safe word to use, so I can decide what *I* like, but when I do use that word, you think I'm rejecting you."

"That's ridiculous." He scowled.

"For once, I'm speaking the truth. *About you.* You're afraid that if you do something I don't like, I'll leave you."

"That's pretty hard to do, considering you're stuck in antiquity."

"But I can go away." She tapped her temple with her index finger. "I can leave you, here, in my mind." She patted her heart. "And here."

He flexed his hand by his side. His look grew dark.

"Did I hit a sore spot?"

He didn't reply.

"I think I did. I also think that you can spank the shit out of me the way you did before, but it still won't give me my heart's desire...or yours." Her eyes stung with unshed tears. "I may be trapped here in this ancient era —" She inhaled sharply, her throat clogging with frustration. "But I still want *total* domination from you."

"You have it, Lyla. I'm your master."

Anger rose within her. *He still doesn't get it!*

She jabbed him in the chest with her index finger. She did it so hard that he was forced to walk backwards, until he ended up at the writing table. It shook when he bumped it.

"Let me tell you something Mister Roman Alpha Male." She poked him again. "I may be a kinky, modern bitch, but I still want to be swept off my feet by a man who commands my body and soul."

"What is this 'swept off your feet'?" He looked around. "I see no broom."

"Oh, Marcus," she sighed. "It means that I want you to surprise me."

He angled his head. "In what way?"

"I want to be bowled over — when you punish me, and in your complete and total domination."

* * * *

183

Marcus stood there, afraid to move. He couldn't believe his ears, or his good fortune. Perhaps, the ancient Roman myth of gods and goddesses was true. Maybe, Cupid and Aphrodite had joined forces, and deigned to shower him with happiness.

He couldn't contain his excitement, or his desire for Lyla.

She had finally expressed something to him that would take their relationship to a different level, and while he would enjoy her total submission, he feared it too. It would bind her to him so that he wouldn't be able to just use her as his lupa, she'd have to become more.

His woman. One he must protect and cherish forever.

She stood before him, her head bowed in supplication. "I'm sorry for what I did, for what happened to Appia," she whispered. She didn't look up, dropping to her knees before him. "I want, no I require, more punishment, Master."

Master. Her voice sounded humble.

He didn't have to wrench the word 'Master' from her, or command her to say it.

"May I look at you?"

"Yes, you may."

She raised her eyes to his. "Will you use the whip?" Her voice became small, yet it held seductive notes.

The two aspects of Lyla's personality sucker punched him in the gut.

He bent and clasped the back of her head, gasping when her lips sought his cock.

"Please," she whispered. "If you do not punish me properly, how will I ever learn, Master?" She continued to suckle him, her hot, moist mouth making him shudder.

He was tempted to toss her over his lap again for driving him mad with need. His eyes almost rolled back in his head when she kissed his balls. Such a sweet, tempting morsel was his Lyla.

"Rise," he commanded. Meting out her proper punishment filled him with lust. His gut burned with it.

She rose, but she didn't meet his eyes.

Ah, the perfect, submissive mate.

"You're going to receive exactly what you deserve, my sweet."

"Yes, Master." She bowed her head lower.

"Your punishment will commence, but you'll know neither the time, or day, or what implement I will use."

"I cannot choose?"

"No. You have no say in this, Lyla. None at all."

"Oh."

"You will remain in your room until I am ready for you."

She nodded.

A slow smile spread across his face. "Until it's time for you to be well and duly chastised."

Chapter Twelve

Sometime later, Lyla sat on the bed in her room, her knees drawn up to her chest. It seemed like the only position she could stay in that would contain her anxiety...and her excitement.

The idea of Marcus whipping her ass made her flush. It fuelled her anticipation. Her body throbbed with it.

A loud knock sounded through the room. Lyla glanced towards the entrance to her room. In the next instant, Appia entered, turning to slide the door closed.

Lyla arose and greeted her.

"I understand you're to be punished by his Excellency," Appia stated.

Lyla blew out a breath. "That's correct."

"But why?" She placed a hand on Lyla's arm, giving it a gentle squeeze.

"I'm going to begin by saying that I watched you receive your punishment."

"How could you have..." Appia nodded. "Ah, the peepholes."

"I just happened to be in Marcus' room," Lyla continued, her words coming out in a rush lest she lose her resolve. "I heard you speak, then I watched it all. While I didn't understand what you and Marcus spoke about, later, when you and I discussed everything, I realised that what I'd witnessed is punishment that I should have received."

"Oh, Lyla, I told you that I deserved it. Stealing from the master was a foolish choice on my part."

"I want you to know that I told Marcus that I filled your head with notions about not marrying Cletus."

Appia frowned. "The master didn't have to know. What did it matter who told me not to marry Cletus, I—"

"It mattered to *me*, Appia. I-I was jealous of your transformation. So envious of what you are going to share with Marcus' friend." She sighed. "I also didn't want to come to terms with how kind Marcus can be."

Appia smiled. "He is a firm but fair master. His friend Cletus is, too." Her grin turned a bit wicked. "Cletus is very handsome. I wish you had met him."

"Maybe I will some day." Lyla patted her hand.

"Marcus Flavius Valerius will not break your spirit." Appia nodded. "He loves you."

Lyla's heart beat wildly.

"He has found a perfect mate in you." Appia's smile widened.

Lyla reached out to embrace her.

Appia returned her hug. "Be brave when you receive your chastisement," she whispered.

"That's easier said than done."

Appia winked. "I would bet all of my coins on you."

* * * *

A short time later, Marcus left his bedchamber, dressed in regal splendour. He wanted to make an impression on Lyla that would last a lifetime.

They were thrown here together in his ancient era for a purpose, and no one and nothing would keep him from her. He'd chase her across time if he had to.

The ornator adjusted the toga on Marcus' shoulder, pinning a large, ruby-red brooch to the material. Marcus planned to give the jewellery to Lyla... That, and so much more.

Time was such a precarious, strange thing. Sometimes, it dragged, like when he anticipated holidays and birthdays as a boy. Other times, it flew by, especially when he was with Lyla.

He wanted her in his bed, a willing supplicant. In this time, or any other.

He left his room, anticipation burning through his gut.

Decimus greeted him, walking towards him. "You are quite the royal sight today, Excellency." He bowed. "Do you have a few minutes for me?"

Marcus was eager to bring Lyla before him for her chastisement, but the worried look on Decimus' face made him give in. "What's troubling you?" He placed a hand on the elderly servant's shoulder.

"Rumors are rife today in Rome."

Marcus sighed. "As usual, Decimus."

"Yes, but these concern Corvus."

"*What?*"

"I hear he's seeking revenge for what you did to him."

Marcus fingered his jaw, remembering the blow received from Corvus' lackey when he and his men raided

Corvus' prison. He'd brought Corvus to his knees for what he did to Lyla.

"I bid you to be careful, Excellency, and watch your back. Your feud with the slave dealer may escalate."

"Keep your eyes and ears open, Decimus. I want all news about Corvus and his plans."

The old servant bowed. "It shall be done."

* * * *

Lyla took her time in the bath, allowing Eisha and Corinne to attend her. They scented her body with rose oil then dressed her in an exquisite, deep red silk gown. Adorning her upswept hair with tiny rosebuds, they placed them strategically on her head so that they stood out against her pale tresses and creamy white skin.

Their actions made her feel special, like a queen, and like royalty, she must be valiant.

Whatever Marcus planned for her, she'd take. She wanted to be his fearless girl and his submissive mate. He may be her Master, but she possessed the control. It would be her choice how she took her punishment.

She wouldn't let him down. Or herself.

Four eunuchs escorted her, Eisha and Corinne from the baths to the room where Marcus kept his whip collection.

Which one would he use? Sweat beaded on her upper lip while she thought about it.

Eisha and Corinne bowed before her.

More than anything, she wanted Marcus to understand that what she was about to do was for them both.

She knocked on the door then heard Marcus' deep voice. "Enter."

She hesitated for just a second, the deep timbre of his voice almost undoing all her resolve.

Corinne slid the door open so that Lyla could walk into the room she so loved. The crops and whips greeted her, but her eyes settled on Marcus. He stood tall and proud, regal in his red silk toga and snow-white tunic.

"Kneel," Marcus commanded, pointing his index finger at the ground.

She dropped to her knees before him.

He walked over to her and raised her chin using his index finger. In a low voice, he said, "You look exquisite, my sweet."

She crossed her arms over her breasts, forming an X. She became invincible, despite her supplicant pose. It was the first time since she arrived in this ancient time that she truly felt alive and in control. Maybe it was the very first time she'd *ever* experienced that.

"I intend to give to you everything you deserve."

Her little pleasure bud sprang to life. Moisture seeped down her thigh.

"Strip," he commanded.

Outside, a commotion ensued. She heard loud voices. One by one, Marcus' household filled the room. Lyla lifted her eyes to see all the men and women who had attended her since she arrived. Corinne and Eisha stood on the side. As well as Appia.

He's going to punish me before an audience!

She'd give him, *and them,* the greatest spectacle they'd ever witnessed. But first, she had to tap her inner core of strength and eradicate her fear.

"Strip," he commanded, "or I will do it for you."

She took a deep breath and clapped her hands.

Eisha and Corinne walked over and helped her to her feet. With slow, careful movements, they slipped the gown downward, revealing her breasts. They pushed it further until her waist, hips, and thighs came into view. A final tug sent it to the floor.

She stood naked amidst a red silk pool swirling around her ankles.

"Magnificent," Marcus whispered in her ear. "You are stunning, my precious one."

Eisha and Corinne bowed before her then quietly took their place with the assembled group.

The sound of wood scraping the tiles caught her attention.

Slaves had brought in a long, narrow wooden table, with two smaller wood pieces attached to the sides. It resembled a modern-day padded redwood picnic table with attached seats.

"Your disobedience will be addressed," Marcus told her. He clapped his hands.

Two slaves stepped forward. They helped her onto the top of the 'table', spreading her legs so that her knees rested on the two lower portions. The slaves then shackled her legs to the bench using chains. They clamped restraints over her wrists as well.

She tugged on the chains, realising that they were padded on the inside, but she was bound just the same. She could not escape from whatever Marcus planned.

He chuckled. "My sweet little fighter. All the way to the *end*." He swatted her bottom, his fingers hitting the bit of her pussy that showed from behind. The sting from her ass started a pleasure tailspin.

Knowing that others watched, heightened the experience. Lyla gasped when something brushed her clit.

"It is a dildo, my sweet." Marcus sat down on the bench near her. "Each time you receive punishment, your legs and arms will move. The table will shake, too. The dildo beneath you is attached to a mechanism that will kiss your luscious cunt each time you receive a blow to your backside." He lowered his voice. "No one knows the dildo is there but me...and you. The others just think you're strapped to a spanking bench."

Her face burned with shame to hear him talk to her that way.

"But I will know if you come. And so will you. I have rigged the mechanism in a certain way to give you pleasure when you move your feet and hands. It will take great strength and will on your part to not come until I command you to do so."

To spite him, she wouldn't move any appendage. Not if she could help it.

"I had to remember the promise I made to surprise you, so I chose the instrument myself."

He clapped his hands. A slave brought forth a long paddle.

Lyla's mouth hung open. He had totally turned the tables on her! Her clit throbbed violently at the sight of that paddle.

"It is smooth to the touch, but will render your bottom a nice red shade," he mused, running the paddle's length along her ass. He lifted the paddle, bringing it closer to her face so that she could view it.

She had to do everything in her power not to lick her lips.

"See the small holes along the sides? You will hear the air whisk through them when I bring the paddle down on your ass."

He'd heightened her senses of touch, sight and sound. In that moment, she realised how truly sensual her Master could be.

Moisture dotted her thighs. She rubbed her nipples against the smooth padding of the spanking bench, causing her moist, heated thighs to quiver in response.

"You will need a strong front, and an even stronger inner core to experience the ultimate pleasure. If you come now, I will know how weak you truly are."

She gritted her teeth.

"Now, for the last, but not least. You will view yourself getting the chastisement you deserve."

He clapped his hands twice. Slaves hauled in two highly polished, tall metal mirrors. They placed one before her, the other, in back.

Lyla saw her reflection in both mirrors. She lay across the bench, her ass, and pussy on display for her eyes, as well as his and their assembled audience.

"You will ask for your punishment in Latin so that everyone will understand."

"Yes, Master." She kept her voice as steady as she could.

"Repeat these words. *Ego deprecor ultio ultionis ego mereo mereor.*"

She said in a loud voice, *"Ego deprecor ultio ultionis ego mereo mereor."*

"You have just asked for the punishment you deserve. If you're not up to the challenge, say so now."

"The hell I will."

He nodded, pride lining his face. "Very well then, we will commence with your chastisement."

He moved behind her. Standing to the side, he raised the paddle high. A whistling sound made its way to her ears, then the paddle's sting landed on her 'sweet spot', where her ass and thighs met.

The table shook when Marcus struck her bottom. She gripped the chains on her wrists and ankles, instinctively yanking them upward. The dildo pushed into her cunt, vibrating against her clit. Her eyes nearly rolled back in her head from the exquisite, sweet torture it wrought on her.

She heard the air whiz through the holes on the paddle. Then he smacked her again.

The next swat brought tears to her eyes, and a pink blush to her bottom cheeks. In the mirror she saw the reflection of everyone watching. Some slaves smirked, while others, like Eisha and Corinne, stood by, anxiety making their beautiful faces taut.

Appia inclined her head, but not before Lyla noticed her wink. It filled her with the strength to carry on. It also made her wonder if Appia truly enjoyed punishment, as well.

The next smack came without warning, the paddle's sting worse than before. The heat in her bottom, combined with the vibrating dildo made her want to come right there.

He raised the paddle higher. She shut her eyes tightly, knowing it would hurt like the very devil.

"Do you require more?"

"Yes, Master!" She gritted her teeth as pain, humiliation and pleasure mingled together within her body.

Her body shook. So did the dildo. She couldn't come, not yet, damn it.

Her reflection in the mirror showed a cherry-red backside. She wiggled it, her brazen display telling Marcus, and the world, that she could take more.

He bent and whispered in her ear, "Remember your safe word. Use it if you have to."

"Not on your life."

He spanked her backside three more times. The last swat did her in. The dildo pulsated against her pussy, making her want to slip into a deep abyss filled with sexual gratification. Pinpricks of light danced before her eyes while her cunt let go, her release so deep it consumed her.

Marcus tossed the paddle aside and unchained her, but she couldn't move. He lifted her from the bench, sliding her down his body to stand before him.

Lyla's knees gave out. He lifted her in his arms, cradling her stinging backside against his muscled forearm.

"You're disappointed?"

"No," he told her, his voice deep. "I'm filled with pride for your first time on that spanking bench. I didn't think you could hold out as long as you did, but *you* surprised *me*."

She gave him a little smile and tightened her hold around his neck. Nuzzling her face into the warm skin of his throat, she said, "Then we both were swept off our feet."

He slid his bedchamber door open and deposited her on the bed, easing her down onto the mattress. She sat on her stinging butt cheeks, enjoying the heated sensation. She suddenly wanted something very badly.

His cock in her ass. It would be the ultimate humiliation and pleasure.

She lowered her eyes and begged, "Please, Master, I want, no, I *need*, your cock in my ass."

"Are you positive that's what you want?"

"Yes, Master."

Marcus stripped his clothes. He turned her onto her belly and patted her hip. "On your knees, my sweet."

She did as he bade.

He reached over for a small ewer, allowing her to sniff the fragrant oil inside. "I use this to soothe my muscles after I exercise. I believe it will help your bottom." He smoothed his oiled hands across her flesh. "It will make your back channel slippery, too." He eased his pinkie into her bottom hole, but stopped near the first joint on his finger.

She wiggled her bottom, allowing the full feeling to engulf her. "More," she breathed. "Give me more."

He pushed his narrow finger all the way in.

She pressed against the delicious invasion of her backside.

Marcus reached around to cup her breasts with his other hand, massaging them to bring her nipples to life with his fingertips. Then his hand slipped to her cunt. He fingered her clit, making her juices flow. "Stay like that." He patted her hip.

She heard a crinkling noise behind her. She smiled to herself, knowing he placed a condom on his penis.

He resumed his position behind her. "Grab the head board," he commanded. "And hold on tight."

First, she bucked, but then, as she grew accustomed to him, she moved her hips to match his rhythm. The slow movement of his cock in her back channel drove her wild.

He reached between her legs and rubbed her clit again, bringing on a release so powerful, she almost passed out.

She collapsed on the bed. Marcus pulled out slowly, but the absence of his cock made her feel bereft.

He slid next to her, taking her in his arms, cradling her hip against his so she would not lie directly on her bottom.

His lips sought her temple. He brushed them across her skin.

"My sweet," he murmured. "My precious one."

Tears welled in her eyes, but they were not from pain...they were from joy.

* * * *

That evening, Lyla cuddled against Marcus, her bottom nestled in his groin. Darkness settled over his bedroom, the light coming from the full moon outside.

Lyla heard animals roaming on Marcus' vast acreage. An elephant's roar heralded a hyena's laugh. A parrot screeched, while a monkey's shrill cry echoed through the night.

She lay awake next to him, enjoying the animals' calls and Marcus' warmth. His cock buffeted her backside, his penis rubbing against her left butt cheek. It made her giggle.

"Why do you laugh?" he whispered in her ear. Then he nipped her lobe with his teeth.

"You're hard again."

"Lyla." His tone filled with exasperation but he smiled just the same. "I've been hard for you ever since I saw you in that bookstore."

"I never imagined making love could be like this."

He took her hand, lifting it so he could place a gentle kiss on her wrist. "Why is that, my sweet?"

"Ever since I got my first spanking by the nuns in school, I've been fascinated with it. I was eighteen at that time, and just about to graduate from high school. There are times when I just couldn't stop thinking about it. How my ass would feel afterwards."

He grinned wickedly. "I had a feeling you were a hellion. You have that look of pure mischief in your eyes."

She fluttered her lashes. "Why thank you."

"Wicked, wicked girl." He laughed, running his fingers through the hair lining her cunt.

She shivered pleasurably, enjoying the tickling sensation.

"You are a treasure, Lyla, and you did well today. You took your punishment like the brave woman that you truly are."

She stretched her hands and arms over her head.

Marcus leant down and suckled her nipples, stroking her between her legs.

"Suck my cunt."

He raised a brow.

"Master," she moaned when he ran his index finger along her damp pussy. "Please suck my cunt."

He held his finger by his nose and inhaled. "Your essence is fragrant." Marcus placed that finger by her nose, too. The sweet, musky odour drifted by her nostrils.

He rubbed his index finger against his middle one. "You're so wet. So responsive." He licked each digit. "And you taste like the sweetest nectar."

He bent his head to suckle her clit. He drew it into his mouth, holding it there between his lips. Then he released it, gliding his tongue along her sensitive skin.

"Oh. My. God." She ground her ass into the mattress. It hurt, but the pain intensified the glorious ecstasy building inside her. Her belly fluttered. Then a sweet ache started in her groin.

He drove his tongue inside her, mimicking what his penis would do.

Her body shook. *That* made everything more intense. "I'm going to come," she moaned.

"Not yet. I want to try something. Are you game, Lyla?"

Was she! Anticipation filled her body. It made her want to come even more, but she held back, wondering what he'd do.

"Arch your back, my sweet, and close your eyes."

She did as he bade, until her breasts were near his mouth. Something hot and spicy touched her lips.

"Open your eyes."

She looked down. A cherry pepper!

The burn entered her mouth, enflaming her tongue and throat. Distracted by the pepper's spicy, hot taste, she gasped when her right nipple stung, too. The burning sensation made her clit pound.

She saw a drop of liquid kiss her nipple. She glanced at the small dish Marcus held in his hand. Filled with diced hot pepper, the juices mingled with tiny yellow seeds. Dipping his pinkie finger into the mixture, he placed another fiery liquid drop on the turgid nipple.

Lyla's mouth opened in surprise. He captured it with his own, kissing her hard, then he did the same thing to her left breast, bringing that lovely burning sensation there, too. It travelled down to her pussy, making it throb even more.

He took his other hand and rubbed her clit. The engorged little bud filled while Marcus dripped the peppers' hot juice on her nipples.

She could not stop her release. A slow smile spread across her face. "Master, I'm coming."

He shook his head. "I thought you could hold out. It looks like I'll have to punish you, for I did not command you to come."

She lowered her lashes. Oh, how she loved this play of domination and submission. Blood totally filled the little fleshy bit between her legs. Her cunt pounded with it. She shuddered from it.

Marcus tucked her against his side, holding her close. His lips grazed her temple. "You're going to get another paddling."

"I know." She yawned.

"But not now. You're too sore."

"I could take it."

His lips settled in her hair. "I'll decide when you're ready."

"Yes, Master." She lowered her lashes in subservience, not daring to look at him, but inside, she soared high on wings of sexual freedom.

"You won't know when your punishment will occur. It will happen when you least expect it."

She cracked one eye open and smiled.

Chapter Thirteen

A little while later, Lyla woke to a rustling noise. When her eyes adjusted to the darkness, she noticed the ancient book lying open on Marcus' writing table. Slowly, the pages turned by themselves.

She rose from the bed, padding over to the book that held her mind and body captive. Her curiosity piqued despite her belief that it was all nonsense.

The book's pages unfurled, fluttering through the air, then they stopped.

Would there be another message? She rounded the corner of the table until she stood over the book. She sucked in a breath and read.

Your journey is complete,
For you've got what you seek.
You may now go home,
To the land where you belong.

She remembered him saying that he couldn't possibly write in the book. Lyla picked up a stylus and tried to scratch over the writing, but some unseen force held her hand above the book and wouldn't let her write.

Slowly, she lowered her hand. It shook.

Her watch sat on the table next to the book. The hands turned clockwise then they spun around the watch face, their breakneck speed making her dizzy. She viewed their frenzied turning, her heart pounding.

The hands slowed, eventually coming to a complete stop. Three o'clock.

It was the same time she had started her perilous journey from the bookstore through that portal.

She sensed Marcus' presence behind her. When she turned to look at him, the moon's soft glow outlined his magnificent form. Her loins stirred.

"Will you go back now?" he asked.

To the land where I belong.

All the things she missed—her creature comforts, her home, her car, electricity, and the sound of modern music suddenly seemed... Foreign.

"I-I should go," she murmured, running a hand over the book's cover. She avoided that bright orange stone.

"Touch the gemma, Lyla. Stroke it upwards. You'll be propelled forward."

"To my own time?"

"Yes."

She raised her eyes to his. "How can you be sure?"

"The message was clear, wasn't it?" His tone was clipped, but his face looked sad.

Clear, yes, but instead of experiencing joy, her heart broke.

I can go home.

Now.

All I have to do is rub that stone.

She pursed lips that turned dry when she thought about going back.

"Don't be afraid, Lyla. I will go with you."

Her eyes widened. "You would really come with me?"

"Yes."

"And leave your home?"

"This would not be home, not without you."

A huge lump filled her throat. "I-I couldn't ask you to do that. To go with me."

"I would go back to the bookstore. Thanks to you and that seminar, I discovered how much I enjoy it."

"Oh, Marcus." Tears formed around that lump in her throat.

"I believe it is what I was meant to do."

She sighed. "But what would happen to everyone here? Decimus said that you're always careful not to mess up the fabric of time. If you left your people—your household—what would happen to them? Wouldn't it alter the time's pattern?"

His face clouded for just a second. "My father left me and my mother, but we managed just fine."

She walked around the table to stand before him. "Did you?" She raised a brow. "I believe that you never forgave your father for travelling to some other era."

"He's happier...wherever he went, that's why he didn't come back."

She thought for a second. "Marcus, did you start time travelling to find him?"

Several seconds went by then he nodded.

"Can you honestly say that you feel good about what he did?"

"I forgave him a long time ago for not coming back."

"But you can't erase the huge hole his disappearance made in your life. Your people couldn't possibly excuse your defection if you came with me. They are your family, especially Decimus. He's been more like a father to you than your own." She reached out and grabbed his hand. "If you abandoned Decimus, he'd be sold to some evil man, like Corvus." She ran a finger along Marcus' chest. "Decimus said you're a good man, because you acquired knowledge when you travelled to the future." She lifted her eyes to his. "Stay here and try to make things better. Besides, running away with me won't erase the pain your father caused you."

He lifted a brow. "When did you become so smart?"

She stood on her tiptoes and kissed him. "Everything I ever knew or learnt came from my very handsome, very brilliant, master."

"You're impertinent." He patted her left butt cheek.

"I'm also right."

A corner of his mouth curved upwards.

"And it's all the more reason that I should stay here, with you," she told him.

"Why is that?"

"To keep an eye on things." She tried to sound flippant.

He didn't say a word, didn't insist that she stay.

Her heart crumbled.

Silence stretched between them.

He cupped her shoulders between his hands and squeezed gently.

"Lyla, you have to realise by now that ancient Rome is fraught with dangers. I can protect you from men like Corvus and my cousin, but the diseases that have been eradicated in your time are present here. You could become sick and die if you were to remain with me."

"That could happen to me back home. There's still plenty that could kill me there."

He scowled, crossing his arms over his wide chest. How she adored those fine, dark hairs that lined the olive-toned skin on his forearms.

"It can happen a lot faster here. There's typhus and cholera and —"

She placed a finger over his lips.

He captured her hand in his. "There would be no modern doctors or medicine to cure you."

"It's my choice to stay, isn't it? You said I wasn't a prisoner."

"You'd become one, because eventually, you'd hate it here. It is better if you return home now."

"Ancient Rome feels more like home to me than my time."

"Lyla," he moaned. He brought her into his arms and kissed her. "I want you to stay. Truly. But for your own sake, you must go back."

She stepped away from him. "No. I won't go."

He flexed his hand by his side. She looked at it and smirked. "Plan on using that on me?"

His hand stilled. "I *should* paddle you, since talking sense doesn't work."

"I've made up my mind." She angled her chin. "Besides, a puny spanking by your hand wouldn't mean anything to me." She reconsidered her flippant statement when she saw the look on his face. She backed up towards the door, but immediately moved away when her back felt as if it were singed.

"What's wrong?" Marcus frowned.

An acrid odour drifted by her nose. She wrinkled her nostrils at the offending smell. Her eyes widened. "Marcus! Look." She pointed towards the door.

She covered her mouth with her hand, while a choking sensation filled her throat. Heat seared her lungs, making it difficult to breath. She watched in horror as a huge cloud of smoke rose from the space beneath the door. The thick haze quickly filled the room.

Her eyes watered. Through the murky darkness, she could barely distinguish Marcus' tall frame. Heat enveloped her body. Beneath the door, she could see the deep red glow of… Fire!

"Get out through the window." He pushed her towards it.

She looked upwards. The opening seemed small. *Would she fit? How about him?*

"Go, now. Before it's too late." Marcus gripped her arm. He made her stand on a bench then he shoved his shoulder beneath her ass. "Grab the ledge," He ordered.

"I'm not going without you."

"Damn it, woman. This is no time to argue. Move." He propelled her upwards until her upper body became level with the window.

She grasped the edge and hoisted herself through the small opening. She looked down. *Big mistake.* Everyone and everything seemed soooooooooooo tiny.

"Go!" She heard Marcus shout.

"I-I can't do this." She squeezed her eyes closed while dizziness washed over her.

"There's a balcony below. I'll ease you down the ledge so you can land on it."

"Come with me," she begged.

"Lyla, go!" He gripped her hands, easing her body over the ledge.

She turned her head to see that Rome had become a smouldering inferno. Every residence, store, and business burned with bright intensity.

She looked down. The people standing on the street under Marcus' window stretched a wide piece of cloth then held it upwards. They shouted something in Latin.

"They're telling you to jump, Lyla."

"Oh, no," she whispered. Her body shook. "I'm not falling onto that thing." It would probably tear. She'd go right through and hit the pavement.

Smoke drifted out the window.

"Lyla, forgive me," Marcus told her. "But it is your only chance to save yourself." He pushed her over the edge.

She slipped away from him.

The last thing she heard as she headed towards the pavement was him calling to her, his voice filled with pain.

Inside the room, Marcus dipped his toga into a basin filled with water. He tossed the long swatch of material over his head and shoulders. Now that Lyla was safe from the inferno, he could determine if anyone else in his household remained trapped inside.

He pushed against the door. It fell away from the frame, landing in the hallway, a mass of flaming cinders. His shoulder grew hot, his skin seared, even though the damp material covered it.

A thick smoke cloud and flames greeted him. His gut twisted.

He'd probably die in this blazing conflagration, but at least Lyla would be safe.

If she made it in one piece to the street below.

Guilt tore at his insides, but what else could he have done? Subject her to the fiery hell surrounding him now?

His eyes watered, making it difficult to see directly before him. Violent coughing ensued. He could barely catch his breath, for his lungs filled with heated air.

Marcus tripped over something on the floor. When he could focus, his eyes beheld Decimus. His guts twisted when he saw Decimus' soot covered body.

Marcus picked him up and heaved him over his shoulder.

"Thank you, Master." The older man could barely speak.

Relief turned Marcus giddy. Decimus was alive! "Don't be so quick to thank me yet, Decimus." His voice sounded gruffer than he'd intended, mainly because he fought back tears. "I still have to get us away from here."

Decimus wheezed, "I would have d-died, M-master, if you hadn't come along."

"Just tell me, did everyone else get out?"

"Yes." Decimus coughed. "But what about Lyla? I-I didn't see her."

"I got her out." Those were the last words Marcus uttered as he ran through the doorway leading to the street.

When he looked back, he noticed the grand entrance of his magnificent residence engulfed in flames. The wood burned quickly, causing the ornate structure to crumble to the ground in a smouldering pile. But they had made it!

He held onto Decimus, but pushing through the crowd was impossible. Chaos reigned. People and animals ran through the streets in a wild frenzy. Roman soldiers tried to keep order, but the crowd rioted. If he could just find Lyla!

"Master, I can walk."

"The hell you can."

A small alleyway came into Marcus' line of vision. He made a right turn, and deposited Decimus behind some large, stone ewers. "Stay here. I will return for you."

"I trust you, Master." Decimus grabbed his hand. "I know you will come back for me." He gripped it tightly. "Master?"

Marcus stroked Decimus' head. "What is it, old friend?"

"Corvus did this. I overheard a rumour that his men were going to set your home on fire, but I never had a chance to tell you."

Marcus' ears filled with a buzzing noise. Rage engulfed him. If he got his hands on those bastards, he'd slaughter them like the animals they were. They burned his home, and set fire to all of Rome, too!

Decimus slumped against the urns.

Marcus got down on his haunches. He saw that Decimus' chest rose and fell, but his breathing seemed shallow. Marcus removed his toga and wadded it into a ball, placing it beneath Decimus' head.

"Sleep," he whispered to Decimus, stroking the elderly man's shoulder. "I will come back for you."

Marcus' eyes watered. His chest tightened. He didn't want to leave, but he had no choice while he searched for Lyla. Decimus would slow him down.

He got up and ran through the streets, pushing and shoving his way through the crowd. He stopped dead in his tracks when his eyes beheld a man hoisting Lyla onto his horse. She kicked and screamed, but the man didn't release her, slapping her across the face to silence her cries.

From where he stood, Marcus swore he could see blood flow over Lyla's mouth.

His blood ran cold, filling him with icy rage.

She writhed and twisted, but the man ignored her attempts to free herself.

Marcus growled low in his throat, his fury unleashed. "Lyla!" He tore down the street, adrenaline pumping through his veins.

She couldn't possibly have heard him, but he continued to call her name.

Marcus skidded across something wet and slimy. Regaining his balance, he looked down and saw what caused it.

A Roman soldier lay face down on the cobblestone pavement, his throat slashed. Blood pooled around him, flowing over the rough stones.

Marcus ignored the gory sight. He reached for the sword that remained in the man's fisted hand. The poor bastard never had a chance to use it.

Marcus swung it before him, waving and shouting as he ran. The crowd parted. They had no choice, lest he mow them down in his fury and need to get to Lyla.

* * * *

Lyla had bounced once on the stretched linen, grateful she didn't fall or rip through the fabric. Cracking her stupid head on the pavement would have been such a ridiculous way to die. A hysterical little giggle escaped her throat.

Focus!

Don't think about anything but finding Marcus.

He had to have escaped the inferno... "Please be alive, Marcus. Be alive!" But when she saw his residence, her heart plummeted.

His beautiful home had burned to the ground. What remained still blazed, the flames darting through the windows.

"Marcus," she cried. "Oh, Marcus." She placed a shaking hand against her lips. Running through the crowded streets near his home, her grief morphed into fury.

Who did this horrible thing? What idiot left a candle burning, or...

Soon, she became entrenched with the crowd hurrying away from Rome's interior. Occasionally, Lyla would glance upwards to see burning wood fall onto the street.

A woman shrieked, a child screamed in pain. Lyla helped them to their feet, her arms shielding the small girl from the wood's fiery embers. The hair on her arms singed, but she didn't care because her body had become numb with grief over Marcus. The woman mumbled something in Latin, her face awash with tears. She grabbed Lyla's hand and kissed it, but cinders rained down on her skin. Ash coated the fine hairs lining her arms.

Lyla pushed her way through the crowd and pressed her body against a wall while people passed her by. No one gave her a second glance. All had escape on their minds.

Her knees buckled, but she braced her back and hands against the wall, hoping to remain upright.

"Lyla!" A woman's voice pierced her ears.

She glanced down the street to see someone frantically waving.

"Lyla! Lyla, it's me, Appia."

Before she knew it, Appia materialised before her.

Lyla shook her head, not quite believing it was she. It couldn't be... "Why aren't you on your way to Greece?"

A tall, blond man approached Appia, his face a tight mask filled with anger. He reached for her and hugged her tight, leaning down to shield her from the falling cinders and ash. Then he grabbed her shoulders and gave them a shake, speaking rapidly in Latin.

Appia tried to get a word in, firing off more Latin when she could. "Cletus, est Lyla."

Cletus released Appia, his face red. He said something to Lyla in Latin.

"He is pleased to meet you," Appia translated.

Suddenly, he looked upwards, his eyes widening. He grabbed Appia and Lyla, shoving them both through the narrow opening in an alleyway.

A huge chunk of burning wood hit the ground near Lyla's feet.

He asked Appia something. She nodded.

Appia grabbed Lyla's hand. "Are you all right?"

"Y-yes," Lyla responded, barely. She glanced at Appia. "Why aren't you on that ship bound for Greece?"

"When we heard about the fire, Cletus feared for Marcus and his household. So did I. We came back to see Marcus' house burning."

Lyla's stomach knotted when she thought about Marcus trapped in the fire. Tears filled her eyes.

Just then, a low moan drifted by her ears.

"Did you hear that?"

Cletus shifted his head too, his right ear aimed in the direction from which another low, agonised whimper came. He gave a pointed look to Appia then barked what sounded like a command. He walked over to some large, stone ewers and glanced behind them.

"Decimus." Is all Lyla heard.

Appia walked over to where Cletus stood. "Oh my, *it is* Decimus!"

"But what's he doing *there*?" Lyla joined them, peering over Cletus' broad shoulder.

Soon all three were helping Decimus to his feet.

"The M-master made me r-rest here while he searched for you," Decimus managed to say. His body shook.

Cletus bent and snatched a red toga from the ground.

"It's the Master's," Decimus replied. "He wanted to make me comfortable." He glanced at Lyla. "He is searching for you."

Tears poured from her eyes. Marcus had escaped the fire. And trust Marcus to aide someone else before himself. *I have to find him! I have to!*

She ran blindly into the crowd.

Appia, Cletus, and Decimus shouted her name. She barely heard them such was her need to see her Master again.

She made it back to the street. More people and animals filled the pavement. The soldiers attempted to control the fracas, but it wasn't doing much good. The crowd clawed at the horses the soldiers rode. Some tried to dislodge the men from their seats.

Blood soaked the ground as the army hacked their way through, their swords flying.

Cletus finally caught up with her. He spoke to her in Latin, but the only word she could decipher was Marcus.

Appia joined them and translated, "He says that Marcus wouldn't want you to be in danger. You must stay with us."

"I have to find him. I have to." Lyla grabbed Cletus' tunic. Hot tears poured down her face.

"Then we will all go." Appia nodded.

Decimus added. "Yes, all of us." He almost slid to the ground, but Appia caught him, placing an arm around his waist to steady him.

Cletus' voice turned firm. "Haud, subsisto hic. Ego mos quaero Marcus." He started to shove them all back through the small corridor.

"He wants us to stay here, Lyla," Appia told her. "Cletus said that he will search for Marcus himself."

Lyla could stand no more.

"Lyla!" She thought Appia called her, but when she looked back, she saw Eisha and Corinne.

She stopped long enough to greet her ornators. Then she shoved them against a wall when three Roman soldiers came racing by on horseback. She didn't like the look in the men's eyes. They had murder in them.

"Marcus. Have you seen him?"

Eisha and Corinne just stared at her, fear in their eyes.

Lyla didn't get a chance to utter another word. Her feet left the ground while a man tossed her face down across a horse's back.

A rough hand grabbed her by the hair. She saw a sword, thinking it belonged to a Roman soldier. Her eyes beheld a man's scarred visage. The disfigurement ran down his face, from his right eye, to his cheek. His breath smelt foul. His teeth were rotted.

Corvus' man! He laughed snidely.

She kicked and screamed, but her efforts proved futile.

Soon, two other mounted men joined them. One had Eisha, and the other had Corinne.

He slapped Lyla across the face. Her eyes stung. Her lips numbed, then hot pain shot through her jaw.

They took off at breakneck speed, the horses' hooves beating against the pavement, dodging the burning wood that rained down upon them.

She swayed once, but remained upright enough to turn her head and see Cletus and another man running after them. Her eyes widened in horror while they grabbed the horse's reins and butchered the two men who'd captured Eisha and Corinne. Lyla shuddered in fear, watching Eisha's and Corinne's captors fall from their horses, their throats cut to the bone.

Cletus controlled the horse Eisha rode, pulling her down from the animal's back.

The other man did the same with Corinne, then he turned his attention to Lyla.

Lyla fervently wished she could see his face, but he was covered head to toe with soot. Half naked, his tunic shredded to the waist, his powerful chest muscles strained with every step he took towards her. His hand held the handle of a long sword. The metal glinted in the light from the flames. He lifted it high in the air, his eyes filled with murderous rage.

She struggled to get away, but her kidnapper held her in an iron grip once more.

The crazy man would kill her! She'd never find Marcus, never see him again...

She braced herself to feel the sword pierce her flesh. In the next instant, her captor released his hold. He toppled from the horse and landed on the ground on his back.

Cletus grabbed the horse's reins, calming the animal down.

Lyla saw her captor sprawled on the ground face up, his eyes wide and unstaring, a sword lodged in his chest.

Lyla slipped from the horse. The soot-covered man caught her deftly in his arms. When she looked into his eyes, she recognised him instantly… "Marcus!" She threw her arms around his neck and squeezed him tight.

Cletus soon joined them with Eisha and Corinne in tow. Lyla looked into the street to see their kidnappers lying in their own blood. Soon, a curious crowd gathered around them. She shuddered from fear and from a numbing coldness creeping along her spine.

Marcus cuddled her close. "My sweet. My precious one." His deep voice filled her ears. It drifted through her mind and soul.

"Marcus," she whispered. "Marcus," she repeated, stroking his face. "Marcus." She clutched his shoulders, not quite believing that he was real.

The soldiers slowly restored order. People formed bucket brigades and doused the flames that still leapt from the windows of stores and houses.

Appia and Decimus made their way through the crowd to join Lyla, Marcus, Cletus, Corinne, and Eisha.

Cletus placed an arm around Appia's shoulders and hugged her tightly. Then he draped his toga around Marcus' shoulders.

"Gratias ago vos , meus amicus." Marcus nodded. He spoke rapidly to Cletus, his voice tight, like he held back emotion.

"Oh, Appia, what are they saying?"

"Marcus asked Cletus why he came back."

Lyla watched Cletus grin when he answered Marcus.

"Cletus just said, how could he leave his good friend in such dire straits? Besides," Appia gave her hand a squeeze, "I would have given him no peace until he agreed to return to Rome."

Tears sprung to Lyla's eyes.

Marcus and Cletus finished their conversation. Cletus raised a brow and gave Lyla a wry look.

Marcus smiled, hugging her tightly. He answered Cletus, then spoke in English to her. "He said you are a handful to deal with, but not unlike his Appia."

She cuddled closer to Marcus. "I am shameless, when it comes to you. I would do anything I could to stay right here with you."

Eisha and Corinne helped Decimus walk towards them, supporting him around his waist with their arms. The older man grabbed Marcus' hand and kissed it.

Lyla's chest grew tight with unshed tears when she saw Marcus stroke his hand through Decimus' hair.

She jumped when a loud trumpet blast filled the air.

"The soldiers are commanding us to make way for the emperor," Marcus explained.

Domitian rode towards them a white steed, his tall, arrogant form rising from the horse's back. The crowd parted as he passed, his soldiers keeping a watchful eye. One of Domitian's men shouted something. Before long, everyone knelt before him.

Domitian addressed Marcus.

All Lyla understood was the word Corvus.

Domitian pinched the bridge of his nose, his face contorted by sorrow. "Pardus exuro pessum."

A collective gasp rose from the crowd.

"What's he saying, Marcus?" She looked around. "Why is everyone so upset?"

"The Pantheon has been burned to the ground, Lyla."

"Oh, my!" She placed a shaking hand over her lips.

Domitian spoke again, his voice raised and angry, "Corvus ero punitor!"

"If Corvus caused this, then he will be punished," Marcus translated.

"Corvus." She balled her hand into a fist at her side. "He *should* be punished if he caused this fire."

"He wanted revenge, to burn my home with me in it, but he set the entire city on fire."

Her shoulders slumped when she took in all the destruction.

Domitian spoke to Marcus again and extended a hand towards him. Marcus kissed Domitian's ring. Then Domitian did the same with Cletus. Cletus knelt and kissed Domitian's ring, too.

Marcus and Cletus bowed their heads and said, "Dominus et deus."

Domitian raised a haughty brow then left with his soldiers in tow.

"Appia," Lyla gripped her hand. "What did Domitian say?"

"He called Marcus and Cletus 'Sons of Rome'." Her voice filled with excitement. "He credits them with slaying Corvus' men, the ones who kidnapped you, Eisha and Corinne. They are heroes in Domitian's eyes."

"Wow." Lyla shook her head.

"He also wants Corvus found and punished. Domitian will crucify him."

Lyla shuddered at the thought, but knew Corvus deserved it. He had destroyed the beautiful city.

Slowly, Lyla, Marcus, and their friends made their way to what remained of Marcus' home.

He shook his head. "There's nothing left."

Cletus placed a hand on Marcus' shoulder and spoke to him in a quiet voice.

Appia took Lyla's hand. "Cletus just told Marcus that you are all welcome to come with us to Greece. My family would welcome you with open arms."

"You could rebuild your home, Marcus." Lyla threaded her arm through his. "I'll help you."

Marcus drew Lyla away from his friends. "Listen to me, my sweet. It will be a very difficult existence." He sighed. "I wish I could send you back to your time, at least I would know you'd be safe there."

"You wish to..." She furrowed a brow. "What are you saying, Marcus? That you don't want me?" Her eyes filled with tears.

He grabbed her shoulders. "Lyla, I want you more than my own life."

Her heart soared.

"But the book with the magic stone is gone. There is no way now for you to get home to your time."

Her eyes widened. "So what you're saying is, I'm stuck here forever. Is that it?"

"Yes. Trapped here, in this time, with me."

She hugged him tight. "Oh, Marcus, that's wonderful!"

He shook his head, wonder lining his handsome countenance. "After all you've been through. You still want to be with me?"

She stroked her finger across his jaw and grinned. "Yes, Master, I do."

He took her face in his hands and kissed her on the lips. Then he released her, frowning all the while. "You should have remained in that alleyway with Cletus. He told me you disobeyed him."

Oh, how she adored his commanding tone! "When do I *ever* do as I'm told?"

"You need a good spanking." He grinned, his lips spreading against her temple. Then he sobered, his face tight with anxiety. "Will you really stay here? With me? You could go with Cletus and Appia to Greece. You'd have a better chance surviving there."

"When I thought I had lost you, it occurred to me that if I didn't have you, it wouldn't matter where I was." Her lips trembled. "If I can't be with you, then time has no meaning, in fact, nothing does." She shook her head, her chin at a defiant angle. "I have no intention of going to Greece, and you can't make me."

"Lyla," he breathed her name. "Lyla. *Lyla.*" He hugged her tightly to his chest.

"I love you, Marcus."

"You don't know how I've longed to hear you say that." He captured her face between his hands. Drawing her towards him, he pressed a kiss to her forehead. "I adore you, my sweet, precious one. You are my love, too." His voice deepened. "But you're going to learn to do as I say." He gave her a look filled with dominating, sensual allure.

He loved her!

"I should still spank you."

She couldn't resist getting in the last word. "I'd rather stay here and feel my Roman's hand than be anywhere else." She grinned.

Marcus picked her up and twirled her around, his shout of joy and laughter, echoing through Rome...and time.

About the Author

I sank my writing teeth into my first romance novel after years of reading my favourite authors…Linda Howard, Karen Robards, Kat Martin (just to name a few!) Those ladies inspired me to write my own romances and now, it's my passion.

I'm fascinated by the paranormal…I love to be scared. Ghost stories are my favourite. As a child I read 'The Haunting of Hill House' by Shirley Jackson (it was made into a movie a couple of times…a good one to watch with your favourite honey…and cuddle up to when it gets real scary!) That book made me want to write ghost stories and heightened my interest in the paranormal. I also enjoy writing spicy, sensual, modern-day romance with an added twist of suspense.

Born in the land of the 'Midnight Sun' (Fairbanks, Alaska), I'm an 'army brat.' When my mother's plane landed at Ladd Air Force Base in Fairbanks (no army base…they had to share with the air force back then!) she didn't want to get off— she and my sister were decked out in heavy winter coats and boots—my mother figured it was always icy cold & snowy in Alaska. Meanwhile, it was summer— and 100 degrees! My father stood there waiting for her on the tarmac in a short-sleeve shirt, shorts & sunglasses. She never forgot the experience—and neither did my father. That summer, my mother said the sun never set—there was 24 hours of daylight. Soon we moved on, and at the tender age of three, my family and I settled on Long Island, where I've resided ever since. Long Island's North Shore 'Gold Coast' is where many of my books & stories take place—it's beautiful! Cliffs that look out over the Long Island Sound…a rocky, sandy coastline where pirates once smuggled in contraband…and fabulous old mansions from 'old money' families abound.

When the hubby and I are not on the go, we're spending time with our two terrific children (now grown) and…our two cats.

Catherine Chernow loves to hear from readers.

You can find her contact information, website details and author profile page at http://www.total-e-bound.com.

Total-E-Bound Publishing

www.total-e-bound.com

Take a look at our exciting range of literagasmic™
erotic romance titles and discover pure quality
at Total-E-Bound.

www.ingramcontent.com/pod-product-compliance
Lightning Source LLC
Chambersburg PA
CBHW050044180626
46810CB00002B/889